Three Days to Sundown

Raymond D. Mason

Three Days to Sundown

Copyright © 2010 by Raymond D. Mason

All rights reserved. No part of this book may be used or reproduced by any means, graphic, electronic, or mechanical; including photocopying, recording, taping or by any information storage retrieval system without the written permission of the publisher/author except in the case of brief quotations embodied in critical articles and reviews.

Raymond D. Mason books may be ordered through authorized booksellers associated with Mason Books or by contacting:

You may order books through:
www.CreateSpace.com
or
www.Amazon.com

or personalized autographed copies from:
E-mail: RMason3092@aol.com

(541) 679-0396

This is a work of fiction. All characters, names, incidents, organizations, and dialogue in this novel are either the products of the author's imagination or are used fictitiously.

Cover by Raymond D. Mason
Printed in the United States of America

Books by This Author

The Long Ride Back
Return to Cutter's Creek
Ride the Hellfire Trail
Brimstone; End of the Trail
Brotherhood of the Cobra
A Walk on the Wilder Side
Night of the Blood Red Moon
The Woman in the Field
Day of the Rawhiders
Last of the Long Riders
The Mystery of Myrtle Creek
In the Chill of the Night
Yellow Sky, Black Hawk
Beyond Missing
Aces and Eights
8 Seconds to Glory
Four Corners Woman
Corrigan
A Motive for Murder
Send in the Clones
Murder on the Oregon Express
Night Riders
Too Late To Live
The Secret of Spirit Mountain
Rage at Del Rio
Beyond the Picket Wire
The Tootsie Pop Kid
Across the Rio Grande
Streets of Durango: The Lynching
A Tale of Tri-Cities
Streets of Durango: The Shootings
Suddenly, Murder
King of the Barbary Coast
Showdown at Lone Pine

Dedication

This book is dedicated to Brian and Brent Sackett as well as the entire Sackett family.
I wish to thank them all for allowing me to use their names in this series of books.
May God richly bless and keep you all in His amazing grace.

(Friends are like arrows in the quiver of one's life)

Three Days to Sundown

Preface

THE WAR BETWEEN THE STATES not only tore the country apart, it tore families apart as well. One such family was the Sackett family in the Abilene, Texas area. John Sackett's identical twin sons, Brent and Brian, went off to fight in the War on opposite sides, while the oldest son, AJ stayed home to help his father run their ranch.

Due to their conflicting views of the War, Brian chose to fight for the North, while Brent pledged his allegiance to the South. Although none of the other family members took sides, Brent felt alienated from them and when the War was over did not return to the family ranch.

Instead, Brent became a deputy sheriff in Crystal City, Texas where he saw an opportunity to make some 'easy' money and took it; knowing full well he was breaking the law. His action and its result put him on the run.

Brian had returned to the family ranch when the War ended and acted as ranch foreman, while the oldest brother, AJ, acted as the business manager. John Sackett oversaw the entire running of the ranch and all the final decisions were his.

Two men who worked for the Sackett's had been stealing cattle, and when they feared they were about to be found out, shot and severely wounded AJ. They pinned the shooting on a man who had just been fired. Brian left the ranch in search of the man falsely accused of shooting

AJ and vowed not to return until he'd brought the man to justice.

The trail led Brian (BJ) towards San Antonio where the accused man had a fiancé. Along the way, Brian passed through Crystal City where he was mistaken for Brent; the man who had shot and killed the sheriff while stealing already stolen money from a freight office holdup.

While Brian was gone, the ranch was attacked by a band of outlaws led by Black Jack Haggerty and his sidekick, Frank 'Four Fingers' Jordan. A trailing cavalry patrol thwarted the attack on the Sackett ranch and most of the gang was either killed or captured. The leaders, however, managed to escape.

Our story begins with Jack Haggerty and Frank Jordan nearing a small town on their way to Sundown, Texas. Haggerty and Jordan were two men folks would be better off giving a wide berth too.

1

THE TWO MEN reined their horses to a halt on a small hill that overlooked the town of Cactus, Texas. They were hot, tired, and hungry which only added to their normally foul dispositions. The shorter of the two men, Frank Jordan, looked down at the small settlement and shook his head negatively.

"Why would anyone want to settle down in a godforsaken place like this," he asked?

"I don't know, Frank; but they sure picked the right name for it...Cactus," Haggerty replied.

"I hope our trip to Sundown ain't a waste of time, Jack," Jordan stated with a slight frown.

"It won't be, Frank. I told you that we need a place where we can hide out and lick our wounds. Folks there will cover for us should any lawmen come snooping around. I have kin there; Sundown is the right place for us now," Haggerty said with a grin.

"How much farther is it to this safe haven of Sundown?"

Haggerty grinned, "Safe haven...about three days; maybe four."

Jordan grinned crookedly, "Three days to Sundown," he said and then noticed Haggerty looking back down the trail. "You still looking for them blue bellies, are you Jack?"

"Yep; I've lived this long because I look over my shoulder as much as I look straight ahead. I don't want someone or something coming up from behind me and catching me off guard," Haggerty replied.

"We lost them troopers a long time ago," Jordan scoffed.

"Have you ever heard tell of the telegraph, Frank," Haggerty snapped? "One message sent ahead can have a passel of blue coats waiting for us."

"Well, there ain't no-body following us. If they telegraphed ahead we'll know soon enough," Jordan stated. "We'll feel better after we get some vittles and a couple shots of mescal in our bellies."

Black Jack Haggerty and Frank 'Four Fingers' Jordan had been riding together for a number of years. Haggerty had formed a couple of gangs over the years and knocked off stagecoaches and banks mostly. They had also robbed freight offices and even a couple of saloons which had actually drawn the biggest posses. His last gang had been broken up by the US Cavalry.

It was Haggerty's idea to hideout in Sundown and to formulate a plan for the next job they'd pull off. He'd have to contact some of his old acquaintances; if any were still around. Both Haggerty and Jordan had a insatiable lust for money and would do anything to get their hands on it.

Jordan was nothing more than a sadistic killer and had killed his share of men, women, and even a child or two. He had no conscience and his eyes showed it; they were dead.

It was said of Haggerty that he'd kill his own mother if she had any valuables and he'd cut her fingers off to remove her rings. A human life meant nothing to either man.

They rode down the gentle slope and headed on into the town of Cactus. It wasn't much of a town, but it had the necessities. There was a church, a general store, a feed store, a blacksmith shop and stable, a land office, a gunsmith shop, a bank, a sporting house, two saloons, and a sheriff's office.
As Haggerty and Jordan rode down the main street, it seemed that every pair of eyes were trained on them. It made Haggerty a little nervous, but didn't seem to bother Jordan in the least. Jordan's lack of concern bothered Haggerty.
"Frank, haven't you noticed how everyone is staring at us as if we had wanted posters wrapped around our hats," Haggerty asked?
"Yeah, I've noticed. These people probably don't get many strangers passing through their 'Podunk town'. They'll be..." Frank started to say, but cut off their conversation in mid sentence when he saw the town sheriff walk out of his office onto the boardwalk ahead of them.
Haggerty noticed also, "I see him," he said. "We'll soon know if he's received a telegram or not."
"If he comes our way I'm goin to gun him," Jordan stated with a frown.
"No, wait and see what he wants before you draw down on him. He may just want to know where we're heading. You let me do the talking if he asks any questions, okay?"
Frank nodded in agreement and mumble his okay as the sheriff moved off the boardwalk and out into the street. As Haggerty and Jordan approached him, the sheriff held up his hand and said, "Hold up there; I'd like to have a few words with you men."

The two men reined up when they rode up to where he was standing. Haggerty said, "Howdy, what can we do for you, Sheriff?"

The sheriff looked them over and then asked, "What brings you boys to Cactus."

Haggerty grinned slightly, "These horses we're riding."

The sheriff's grin faded, "I think you know what I mean by that question."

"Yeah, I know," Haggerty replied still smiling slightly and then added, "We're headed out to California."

"California, eh; where are you from...if you don't mind my asking?"

"I do mind your asking, Sheriff. We're not doing anything wrong; just passing through your one horse town. We ain't figuring on staying here any longer than it takes to pick up a couple of supplies and have a beer or two. So why all the questions," Haggerty snapped.

"We've had a report that two men robbed the southbound stagecoach and shot the man riding shotgun. They made off with quite a haul from one of the passengers, that's why I'm asking all these questions," the sheriff replied with a scowl and his hand resting on his pistol grip.

"Well, we ain't robbed no stagecoach. Don't you have a description of the men?"

"More a description of the horses they were riding than the men. Your horses don't match the description."

"But you're thinking if we're the men, we could have changed horses; ain't that right," Haggerty said.

"That's right; that's what I'm thinking," the sheriff said.

"Well, if we were the holdup men you're taking a mighty big chance confronting us right here in the street like this. What with you being alone, and all," Jack grinned once again.

The sheriff returned his smile, "Not really. You see there have been four rifles aimed at you ever since you reined up here," the sheriff said as he looked at the various hiding places of the men aiming the rifles.

Haggerty and Jordan eyed the four riflemen and then looked at one another. This little one horse town was well protected from any would-be badmen who might be passing through.

"Well, I'm sure glad we're not the holdup men. That's quite a little army you have at your beckon call," Haggerty said and then went on. "What we'd really like, Sheriff is some good grub. We've been eating each others cooking long enough. Can you recommend a good eating house here about?"

"Only have one spot in town; but, it's a doozy; right over there...Eatery," the sheriff said as he pointed it out.

"Anything will beat his cooking," Haggerty said nodding at Jordan.

"Right back at you partner," Jordan replied.

"By the way, what are you men's names, anyway," the sheriff asked?

"I'm Jim Davis and this is Tom Brown," Haggerty said.

"Pretty common name, don't you think," the sheriff said.

"We're just common men, Sheriff. Stick around and you'll see just how common we are," Haggerty smiled.

"If you don't mind I'll go with you to the café over there. I'd like to get a feel for what's happening out yonder," the sheriff said with a wave of his hand towards the horizon beyond Cactus.

"How are we going to refuse that," Jordan said under his breath sullenly.

"You'll find that I'm not all that bad company," the sheriff said as he cast a quick glance in Jordan's direction.

Raymond D. Mason

Jordan looked at Haggerty with a frown that expressed his utter contempt for anyone wearing a badge. Haggerty knew that with Jordan's quick temper it wouldn't take much to set him off. It wouldn't be out of character for Jordan to do something crazy and put them on the run again. Haggerty knew he had to do something to dissuade the sheriff from eating with them.

"We noticed some branding going on as we cut across country, Sheriff. You haven't had any trouble with cattle rustlers around here have you," Haggerty asked curiously, remembering they'd seen some smoke a few miles from town.

"Rustlers...yeah, we've had some cases of some steers being lost or stolen. Where'd you men see this branding taking place:"

Haggerty pointed in the direction from which they'd come, "About three miles back that way."

"I had one of our local ranchers come in just a few days ago and report some missing cattle. It wasn't very many head, so I just thought they might have wondered off and got caught in a bog somewhere. The rancher said he'd lost about twenty head," the sheriff stated.

"Not much good at rustling if that's all they took," Jordan said under his breath.

"What was that," the sheriff asked?

"I said, maybe you ought to take a ride out there and take a look," Jordan said without cracking a smile.

"Yeah, you might be right; maybe I'd better form a posse," the sheriff said thoughtfully.

"It may have been less than three miles back; I'm not sure just how far; not being familiar with these parts," Haggerty added in hopes of hurrying the sheriff along.

"You men don't mind if I don't go to the café with you, do you," the sheriff asked soberly?

"No, we understand, Sheriff. Your job and the law come first. We'll be moving on shortly, anyway," Haggerty said.

"I'd better check this out right away. You said you were cutting across country when you spotted the men branding the cattle; right?"

"Right," Haggerty answered.

"Just where about was that," the sheriff asked?

"Oh, let's see. You know where that old dilapidated barn is alongside the road about two or three miles from here? Well, that's where we came onto the main road, and the branding was taking place about a mile from there," Haggerty said convincingly.

"That would be the Stubbs old barn," the sheriff said.

"You should be able to see our horse's tracks all over the place," Haggerty went on.

The sheriff gave the two of them a wave as he started for his horse. Jordan gave him a return wave, exposing his missing thumb. The sheriff moved towards his horse, but then stopped dead in his tracks. Had he been conversing with two outlaws? He had been; and it was Jordan's stub of a thumb that gave him the clue as to who the two men were....Black Jack Haggerty and Frank 'Four Fingers' Jordan.

The sheriff turned around quickly and went for his gun. Haggerty and Jordan had seen the look on his face and knew he had recognized them. They both drew their pistols with lightning quick speed. Shots rang out and the sheriff clutched his chest. He fell forwards and didn't move.

Haggerty and Jordan didn't waste any time kicking their horses into a full gallop. Shots began ringing out from the various places of hiding of the riflemen. The two outlaws leaned out over their horse's necks to make themselves as small of targets as they possibly could.

13

Bullets cut the air around them, but none found their mark.

Haggerty and Jordan rode hard for over a mile before ever looking back. When they finally did they were pleased to find no one giving chase. Obviously the men weren't prepared to form a posse, not with the sheriff being down anyway.

Jordan looked at Haggerty with a scowl, "What brought that on, anyway," he asked?

"I'd say the sheriff noticed that stub of a thumb and put two and two together," Haggerty replied.

"Oh, come on, Jack, who would figure that out simply because he saw a stub where a thumb should be," Jordan argued?

"Could be he had received word from the Blue Bellies about them being on our trail," Haggerty answered.

Jordan thought for a second and then asked, "Telegraph?'

"Telegraph," Haggerty replied.

2

BRENT SACKETT sat staring across the table at a man wearing an expensive suit of clothes and sporting a Derby hat. The other three men at the table watched intently as the two men studied one another's eyes for any sign he may be bluffing. Finally the man in the Derby spoke.

"Okay, Cowboy...I'll see your fifty and raise you fifty."

A grin almost broke through Brent's poker face, but he held it back and didn't show his approval of the man's bet. Brent was holding four Kings.

"Let's see what you've got, Dude," Brent said as he lay another fifty dollars on the poker pot.

"Three little ladies and a couple of gents to go with them, my boy," the man said as he lay his cards down face up, showing three Queens and pair of Jacks.

Brent grinned slightly as he slowly laid his cards out one at a time. The man in the Derby's smile faded as he watched the four Kings hit the table.

"Four Kings...you've had an amazing run of luck, Cowboy," he said with the distinct sound of disappointment registering in his voice.

"I have at that, Dude. I notice Lady Luck has been fairly good to you today also, though. I see a couple of hundred dollars in front of you there," Brent said.

"Lady Luck never stayed on my shoulder as long as she did on yours, though," the man went on.

Brent looked hard at the man and then said, "Be careful where you're going with this conversation, Dude. I'd hate for you to ruin our friendly relationship here."

"I'm just saying that luck tends to move around the table a little bit more freely than it is today, that's all," the man said.

"Look if you're implying that I'm cheating then come right out and say it. Otherwise, deal the cards and shut up," Brent snapped angrily; his words clipped and sharp.

"I'm not accusing you of cheating...you're not are you?>"

"Now what do you think my answer to that question is going to be, Dude," Brent said with a disgusted look on his face.

"I don't think he's been cheating, Mister," one of the other men in the game stated. "Just deal the cards."

"Neither do I," another player agreed. "Let's play cards."

"How about a round of drinks on me," Brent said as he waved towards a barmaid. "Drinks all around here, honey," Brent called out.

The dude shuffled the cards, but never took his eyes off of Brent. Brent noticed and a frown creased his brow causing him to cast a hard glance at the man's face. When the dude finished shuffling the deck he started to deal.

"Let's see what the bottom card on the deck looks like," Brent said. "You don't mind showing us, do you?"

The other three men tensed as they looked from Brent to the dude and then back at Brent. This was as close to accusing a man of dealing off the bottom of the deck as you can come without actually saying it.

Three Days to Sundown

The dude bristled, "I didn't call you a cheat, Cowboy, and I will not allow anyone to call me one. If anyone is cheating in this game it is the man with the most money sitting in front of him. As we can all see, that would be you."

The sound of Brent's .44 Colt's hammer being jacked back under the table seemed extra loud. Everyone at the table grew totally silent as Brent glared at the dude.

"Is that what I think it is," the dude asked; his forehead breaking out in sweat?

Brent didn't answer immediately, but nodded his head yes in reply. After several tortured seconds he said softly, "Now what was that again?"

The dude's eyes darted from one face to another as he swallowed hard. He slowly raised the deck of cards up so everyone could see the bottom card. It was an Ace of spades.

The tension eased considerably when the sound of the Colt's hammer being let down was heard. The game went on without another incident. When Brent finally walked away he was three hundred and forty dollars richer than when he first sat down. The dude was richer as well...he was still alive.

As Brent walked up to the bar to have another shot of whiskey before turning in, he moved up alongside a man wearing a brown vest. When the man turned and faced Brent the star pinned on the man's vest instantly caught Sackett's eye. He grinned slightly.

"How's it going, Sheriff," Brent said?

"I'm doing okay. I hear there was a little tension at your poker table tonight, is that right," the sheriff asked?

"Oh, there was; I didn't notice," Brent said as he looked away from the sheriff and towards the large mirror behind the bar.

"I heard you prodded the fella in the Derby and fancy clothes. If I was you I wouldn't push him too far. That's

Gentleman Dan Ford; he can be a mean hombre when he takes a notion to be. He gets even with men who call him out during a game of poker," the sheriff said.

"Is that right? Well, if that's the case then I shouldn't have anything to worry about. We parted the best of friends. His problem is that he bets too reckless at times. He's good, but not great," Brent said matter-of-factly.

"I haven't seen you around here before. How long have you been in San Antone," the sheriff asked?

"I just came in yesterday and I'll be leaving in a day or two. Why do you ask?"

"I just like to know these things when I meet a stranger in town. My name is Roy LeBarge by the way," the sheriff said and stuck out his hand.

"Dan Johnson, Sheriff; glad to meet you; it's always good to meet the man who keeps the peace in town," Brent said with a wry grin as he turned his attention back towards the big mirror.

The sheriff turned and looked into the mirror as well. LeBarge watched Sackett's eyes as they both peered at the big glass. Just then a cute little barmaid walked by which caught Sackett's attention.

"Yeah, I'll be moving on as soon as I rest up and get to know a few of your ladies here in town a little better," Brent said.

Noticing who it was who had caught the man who introduced himself as Dan Johnson's eye, the sheriff said, "She's a handful...just for your information. Be careful of her though; she's got a few men stuck on her and they're a little on the jealous side."

"I know the type; besides I've got my eye on the brunette who was waiting on our table," Brent said evenly.

"Mona, she's good. Never causes any trouble and knows her way around tense situations. She's the one who told me about you and Ford's little nose to nose confrontation."

"I'll have to thank her then. The last thing I want is to run into any trouble; especially with the law," Brent said with another wry grin.

"That's what I like to hear strangers in town say. Keep those thoughts and you and I will get along just fine," Sheriff LeBarge said and turned around to go. "Well, I have to finish my rounds. Nice talking to you, Johnson."

"Yeah, same here, Sheriff," Brent said evenly.

Brent watched the sheriff as he walked towards the batwing doors. Just as the sheriff exited Mona, the barmaid who had waited on Brent's table walked by and gave him a big smile. Brent returned the smile and tipped his hat slightly, as he asked, "What time do you get off?"

"Depends on the man," Mona said seductively.

Brent smiled widely. This was his kind of woman.

"We certainly want to thank you for helping us out, BJ," Cletus Cameron said as the wagon loaded with the four prostitutes pulled to a stop in front of the San Antonio sporting house where the four would be working.

Brian (BJ) Sackett had escorted the wagon to San Antonio when they had been ambushed by unknown assailants several days earlier; the assailants may have been unknown to them but had actually been led by Brent Sackett. Brent had not known that his brother was one of the men with the wagon load of women. The two men with Brent had been killed, but one of the men breathed the name Dan Johnson just before he died.

BJ smiled, "Think nothing of it, Cletus; the pleasure was all mine.'

"What do you mean, 'the pleasure was all yours'," Cletus laughed. "You didn't take full advantage of the pleasure that was yours for the asking."

"Well, I guess I'm just a one woman man," BJ smiled.

"G' bye, BJ, you be sure and come visit us before you leave town," one of the women called out to Brian.

"If I can find the time, Annie," BJ called back. "You take good care of yourself."

"I'll take good care of you if you'll come say goodbye," Annie said getting a laugh as well as the same offer from the other three women.

"I'll bet you would," Brian said with a chuckle.

Cletus shook Sackett's hand and once again thanked him. BJ reined his horse around and headed down the street in the direction of the San Antonio Hotel. He figured on staying no more than two days in town before heading on back to the Sackett ranch in Abilene.

Brian had passed through San Antonio over a month earlier while pursuing the man he thought had shot his brother AJ; a man named Myron Selman. Selman had a fiancé here in town and Brian only felt it right to inform her of Selman's death down in Laredo. It wasn't something that Brian looked forward to doing.

Selman had been arrested for shooting a man down in Laredo who turned out to be the Laredo sheriff's brother. The sheriff had arrested Selman and then beat him to death while holding the man in his jail.

Selman had worked for the Sackett's, but had been fired for being lazy. Two other Sackett ranch hands had been stealing cattle and changing the brands, then selling them. Afraid they were about to be found out, the two thieves used the firing of Selman to help them shift the blame for the stolen cattle onto him. They shot AJ Sackett, thinking they had killed him, and then swore that they saw Selman do the shooting. AJ had survived, however, but had remained unconscious, thus sending Brian on a wild goose chase after the wrong man.

While chasing Selman, Brian had been mistaken several times by people who thought he had committed a crime in their community. The perpetrator in each case was none other than Brent. Due to these cases of mistaken identities, Brian had begun to wonder if perhaps Brent had not been killed in the War, like the family had assumed when he didn't return to the ranch. Little did Brian know that his brother was also in San Antonio, and their paths were about to cross again. Only this time it would be in a face to face meeting.

Brian and Brent had been on a collision course for nearly two months and fate was bringing them closer and closer together. Brian (BJ) had begun to consider the possibility that not only was alive, but was a man on the run.

Raymond D. Mason

3

BJ SPUN the hotel register around to sign it, but suddenly stopped with the pen held over the page. His eyes fell on one of the names already in the book; the name Dan Johnson. That was the name one of the bushwhackers had called Brian just before the man died after having been shot by BJ.

"What room is this man in," BJ asked the hotel clerk?

"Oh, Mr. Johnson...he's in room 8 at the end of the hall upstairs," the clerk said with a smile. "Why do you know him?"

"No, I haven't had the pleasure. I have heard that name though and was wondering if it's the same man I've heard about," BJ said.

BJ went ahead and signed the register the way he normally did...BJ Sackett.

When BJ looked up the clerk was peering at him with a slight grin on his face. The clerk nodded vigorously and said, "D'you know something...you could pass for his twin brother. Mr. Johnson has a beard and moustache, but I can certainly see the likeness."

"Really...you don't happen to know where this Mr. Johnson is now, do you," BJ asked.

"No I don't. I do know that he's not in his room. His key is hanging on the hook. We prefer that our guests turn their key in when they're going out. It saves on room keys. You'd be surprised how many keys we have to have made over the course of the year."

BJ grinned, "I'll remember that when I go out."

"Please do," the clerk said.

"Do me a favor and don't tell Mr. Johnson I was asking about him," BJ said. "I want to surprise him."

"You don't have to worry about that here at the San Antonio House. Our motto is, 'Our business is your business, but your business is not ours'. We are very careful about privacy here at the San Antonio Hotel." the clerk said proudly.

BJ hoped the man wouldn't say anything to the man registered as Dan Johnson in case it was Brent. Whether or not the clerk was being truthful about the privacy issue remained to be seen.

BJ went up to his room and sat down on the edge of the bed after making sure the door was securely locked. He laid back and his head had barely touched the pillow and he was sound asleep. Normally a light sleeper, the long laborious journey had finally caught up with him. He slept for twelve hours before finally waking up.

Since BJ had checked into the hotel at around noon, it was now midnight. The sounds coming from the outside told him that there were a lot of cowboys in town. He figured it must be payday and the ranch hands were 'kicking up their heels'.

Wide awake after his sleep, BJ got up and headed downstairs. He would take in a couple of the saloons and see what San Antonio had to offer in way of nightlife. He'd also keep an eye out for this Dan Johnson who was supposed to look like him.

BJ's first stop was a bar called the Texas Rose Saloon and Dance Hall. He went in to the sound of a five piece band playing on the main stage. He grinned as he watched the dancing girls on stage kick their legs up high to the cheers of the onlookers.

Moving through the crowd while casting a casual glance towards the dancers, BJ passed within ten feet of the table where Brent was playing cards. Neither man noticed the other due to the throng of people between them.

BJ moved up to the bar and ordered a drink. He turned and looked out over the crowded room. From where BJ was standing he could see the table where Brent was seated, but could only see the back of his brother's head. Brent got up and went outside for a breath of fresh air and pay a visit to the outhouse in back of the saloon.

Two drunken cowboys at the bar began arguing loudly which caused people in the immediate area to turn their attention towards them. One of the men accused the other of trying to steal his woman, a woman he'd only met that night. Before long the harsh words turned to punches.

BJ watched the two men as they locked up in combat and fell across a table. The two men wound up on the floor where they rolled around, flailing away, but doing no real damage.

Sheriff LeBarge moved slowly through the crowd until he stood over the two cowboys. Slowly shaking his head, LeBarge pulled out his revolver and smacked both men on the head hard enough to render them unconscious.

The sheriff looked around and when he saw two men he knew said, "You boys take these two over to the jail and lock them in the same cell. If they want to continue their fight when they come too, they can do it behind bars."

LeBarge turned and looked at BJ and said, "Saturday night and payday; it's like this once a month."

Looking away briefly, the sheriff suddenly snapped his head back around and grinned, "Oh, it's you Johnson; I almost didn't recognize you since you shaved."

BJ looked puzzled, "Are you talking to me, Sheriff," BJ asked?

"Yeah, I'm talking to you. When we talked earlier you had a beard and moustache. What made you decide to shave?"

"Sorry, Sheriff, you've got the wrong man; my name is Brian Sackett...not Johnson," BJ corrected.

"Well, I'll be switched. I talked to a man earlier today who looked so much like you he could be your twin brother," the sheriff said scratching his head.

"I had a twin brother, but we were separated by the War, if you get my drift," BJ said.

"Yeah, it did that to a lot of families."

"You called me Johnson just now...that wouldn't be Dan Johnson by any chance, would it?"

"Yeah, that's the man's name who I met earlier...Dan Johnson. Do you know him?"

"Nope, but our trails have crossed," BJ said with a frown. "I'd like to meet him."

"Well, there's a good chance you'll meet him. He said he was going to be around for a couple of days before moving on. I still can't get over how much the two of you look alike," LeBarge said.

"If you see him, I'd appreciate it if you didn't say anything about me. I want to meet him, but I'd like for it to be a surprise to him," BJ said.

"Oh, okay...there's not any bad blood between the two of you is there?"

"Not from my side; I can't speak for my brother if he turns out to be this Johnson fella, though," BJ said.

Suddenly the sheriff's facial expression took on a more serious look as a thought came to light. He looked quickly at BJ and let his hand slip down to his pistol grip.

"You said your last name is Sackett, didn't you," the sheriff asked?

"Yeah, I did...Brian Sackett; why?"

"I have a wanted poster on a Brent Sackett. He's wanted for a string of shootings. One of them was the sheriff of Crystal City where he was a deputy," LeBarge said as he slowly pulled his pistol from its holster.

BJ took on a serious look as he thought back to the encounters he'd had with the law while pursuing Selman. Due to the various incidents he'd had on his journey he was almost positive that Brent was still alive. The thought that there were wanted posters on Brent made him feel sick to his stomach.

"Sheriff, I trailed a man who used to work for us on our ranch in Abilene all the way to Laredo; a man we thought had shot another brother of mine. Along the way I passed through a couple of hornet's nests that a man folks mistook me for had stirred up. It has to be this man Dan Johnson...who may very well be my twin brother, Brent.

"If you don't believe my story you can wire the sheriff in Abilene and he'll vouch for me. My father's name is John Sackett and he'll confirm what I'm telling you. If we can find this Dan Johnson I think we can get this whole thing cleared up," BJ said firmly.

"Oh, I'll send a wire to Abilene all right, but I'm going to have to hold you in jail until I get word back from there," Sheriff LeBarge said.

Brian tensed, causing the sheriff to cock the hammer back on his Colt, "Don't do anything stupid now, Sackett. I'll take your hardware just to be on the safe side."

"How long is this gonna take, Sheriff. I don't like the idea of being locked up very long," Brian said with a frown.

"I'll send a telegram tonight, so it shouldn't take very long to get a reply. I'd say by daylight," Sheriff LeBarge answered. "Let's take a walk over to the jailhouse."

BJ turned and started for the door with the sheriff walking three steps behind him. BJ didn't like the idea of being locked up, but knew that the sheriff was only doing what his job called for. He'd have done the same thing if the boot was on the other foot.

Just as Brian reached the swinging doors of the saloon three men entered. The third man was none other than Brent, returning from his trip to the outhouse. When BJ saw his twin brother he stopped dead in his tracks.

The two men's eyes fused together in an unblinking stare down with neither man wanting, or unable, to look away. Neither of the men spoke for four or five seconds. It was Brian who finally broke the forced silence, but muttered barely audible, "Brent."

Sheriff LeBarge turned his pistol towards Brent and ordered him to put up his hands, going by the name he knew him by.

"Hold it right there, Johnson. We have a little situation here and you're coming with us to the jail to settle it," the sheriff said and then asked, "Is this your brother, Sackett?"

Before Brian could answer, Brent replied, "You've got me confused with someone else, my name is Dan Johnson, remember?"

The sheriff shook his head slowly, "That's what you told me it was, but this man has a little different story. Now, let's go on over to the jail and see if we can't sort this whole thing out."

Brent knew there was no way he could wait around until the sheriff did any kind of investigation. He'd have to make a move to get away and do it quickly. Once it was learned he was Brent Sackett he would hang for his misdeeds.

Looking very closely at the two men the sheriff mumbled, "I swear you two must be identical twin brothers."

Brent turned his gaze back towards BJ, "I don't look like this guy," he said quietly.

Brian didn't say a word. If Brent was guilty of the crimes the sheriff had told him about, there was no way he wanted to help slip a noose around his brother's neck.

"Give me your hardware, Johnson," Sheriff LeBarge said holding his pistol on Brent.

"Sure, I want to get this thing cleared up as soon as possible," Brent said as he handed the pistol in his holster over to the sheriff.

Sheriff LeBarge was nobody's fool. He'd been a lawman long enough to know that a man on the run is a desperate man. If one of these men was indeed Brent Sackett he would not want to be detained for long in a jail cell. With the sheriff's office and jail being down the street a ways, he wanted another gun on the men. That's when he saw his good friend Bob Murphy.

"Bob, come here," LeBarge called out to Murphy.

Murphy stopped and looked across the street in the direction of LeBarge and his two prisoners. The smile he was wearing dropped from his face.

"Have you got a problem, Roy," Murphy called back?

"I need an extra gun to make sure neither of these boys bolts on me," LeBarge yelled.

"I'll be right there," Murphy said and started across the unusually busy street for this time of night.

A freight wagon caused Murphy to have to wait until it had passed, which was followed by three cowboys on horseback. Brent knew he had to move fast and this was as good a time as any to make a break for it.

LeBarge had stopped them at the edge of the street and there was an alleyway that cut between the saloon and the building next to it. There were a number of large crates stacked alongside the buildings which would make for good cover.

Brian cast another look at his brother hoping to find the right words to say to him; but before he ever got the first word out of his mouth Brent grabbed his arm and swung him around hard into the sheriff. Both men fell to the boardwalk.

When the sheriff hit the ground his gun discharged, since the hammer was jacked back. The shot echoed loudly down the street causing heads to turn. Brian, being the larger of the two men, fell on top of the sheriff.

Brent made a mad dash down the alleyway, darting around the various crates which made him a much harder moving target. Bob Murphy was still in the middle of the street and unable to get a shot off. By the time he reached the spot where the sheriff and Brian were Brent had disappeared around the back of the saloon.

4

SHERIFF LEBARGE scrambled to his feet and glared hard at BJ for a split second. Bob Murphy ran passed the two men as he gave chase to Brent.

"I guess this tells me who the real Brent Sackett is," Sheriff LeBarge said tightly.

"I'm sorry about this, Sheriff. It surprised me as much as it did you," BJ said as he stood up and brushed himself off.

"I won't be a needing to send that telegram after all. I believe your story, Sackett. It looks like you found your brother, and now I'm going to have to find him, as well," the sheriff stated.

The sound of gun shots sent both men running down the alleyway in the direction of the gunfire. When they rounded the corner of the saloon they found Murphy lying face down. Sheriff LeBarge rolled him over and saw instantly that his close friend was dead.

"I guess your brother had another gun on him. He's just added another murder to his list of crimes, too," LeBarge said sorrowfully as he closed his eyes for a moment.

"Oh no, not another killing," BJ said quietly.

"Your brother's going to be sorry to this when I catch up to him...and I will catch up to him," the sheriff stated, and then added. "I'm going to seal this town up so tight a lizard couldn't get out undetected; as for you, Sackett...you're free to go."

Brian started to say something, but caught himself and choked it off. He didn't want to say anything that might be taken the wrong way by the sheriff, seeing as how he'd just lost a good friend. He headed back to his hotel room.

BJ decided to leave the next morning for Abilene; once he'd informed Selman's fiancé of his death. He wanted to put as many miles as he could between himself and San Antonio in case Murphy had friends who might want to take their 'pound of flesh' from him, if they didn't catch Brent.

Unable to shake the truth about Brent turning bad, his thoughts went back to their younger days when they were so close. What had happened, he thought? Had the War actually caused this change in Brent, or was he like this all the time and the War merely brought it out? He didn't know, but the thought hurt him, and it hurt him bad.

Brian climbed the stairs to his room and unlocked the door. He hadn't left a lamp burning so the only light in the room was what was being cast through the window from the street lamps below.

He lit the lamp and turned around to take off his hat and gun belt. That was when he saw the figure of a man sitting in a chair in the corner. He instinctively went for his gun, but saw the seated man already had a gun pointing at him. The seated man was Brent.

"What took you so long, little brother," Brent asked quietly?

"How'd you know this was my room," BJ questioned?

"A dollar to the hotel clerk gives him a loose tongue. So you made it through the War as well, huh? I figured you would though," Brent said as he redirected the barrel of the pistol away from BJ.

"Why didn't you come back home...we all wanted you to. We still do...if it isn't too late. What's all this about you having shot a sheriff," BJ questioned?

"Not one...two sheriffs. They were in the way of something I wanted; money. I guess I'll be leaving Texas for good. It's too hot for me here. Maybe I'll head out West to California; or maybe head up to Montana; I don't know yet. I just know I can't stay around here," Brent said.

"What was your outfit in the War? We may have been closer to one another than we knew," Brian asked?

Brent grinned slightly, "Outfit...it wasn't an outfit, it was an army. Maybe you heard of us? We were called Quantrill's Raiders. A pretty tough bunch of men, you must admit."

"They were nothing more than outlaws; working both sides of the War and loyal to neither," BJ said with a deep frown.

"That's the only way to fight a war. Why should a man lay down his life for some cause when there's nothing in it for him if his side wins? The politicians will move in and take over and line their own pockets and then hand out money to their cronies," Brent said convinced of his belief.

"You sure haven't done anything to bring honor to the Sackett name. At least you could have thought about Ma and Pa. This is going to break their hearts when they hear about it. One of their sons a common outlaw," BJ snapped.

"Common outlaw, did you say? There isn't anything common about me. I didn't just go off half cocked and shoot a sheriff. I got a bag full of money for my effort. I wouldn't have killed him if he hadn't cornered me and forced a showdown," Brent said in a half hearted attempt to justify his actions.

He then added, "Besides that, I changed my name to Dan Johnson to keep the family name limited to just one shooting incident. I ain't all bad, little brother," Brent said and laughed.

"So have you got a plan for getting out of town? The sheriff is in the process of bottling this town up so tight no one will be able to wiggle. He'll have every road staked out. He's bound and determined to get you for killing his good friend," Brian said, his words sharp and clipped.

"So the guy died, huh? I fired at him just meaning to slow him down. I guess I'm just too good a shot to even miss when I'm trying to. As far as getting out of town, that shouldn't be too hard to do. I'll make it out somehow," Brent said confidently.

As an afterthought Brent asked, "What brings you down here, anyway? Are you buying cattle for Pa?"

"I was on the trail of a man we thought was responsible for shooting AJ, but it turned out that the man was framed. They got the guys who actually did the shooting. In case you're interested...AJ is okay," Brian said with a frown.

"I hope he doesn't have any lingering effects of the shooting. It can be rough going," Brent said thoughtfully.

"You sound like you know that from experience," BJ said.

"I do. I caught a ball in the shoulder during one of our raids. Lucky for me the man who shot me was almost out of range; it didn't take much to get the slug out, but it still gives me trouble once in awhile. There may still be a piece of the slug in there."

Just then there was a commotion out on the street causing Brent to move to the window to see if he could see what the noise was all about. A dozen men had gathered and were all carrying torches. Sheriff LeBarge was giving orders to the men and telling them where he wanted them to search.

"It looks like I'm going to have to get a move on, little brother," Brent said as he watched the goings on below.

"Why don't you turn yourself in, Brent? You're only going to make things worse if you continue on down the road you've chosen. You don't want to wind up like the Daltons or the Younger brothers do you?" Brian said seriously?

Brent looked at his brother through hard, cold eyes with just the hint of a grin. He slowly shook his head negatively, "Listen to you. You may be content punchin' cattle all day, everyday; bustin your hump for peanuts, but not me. I'm going to taste as much of life as I can before I pack it in. I'll get out of this mess and when I do I'll have enough money to live like a king.

"I live high, wide, and handsome and it's the kind of life I want to live. Tell the family anything you want to; tell them I'm dead. Or tell them I've lost my mind, I don't care. You can say what you will about the life I've chosen, but I call it exciting. Never a dull moment, and that's the way I want it. I'd rather be dead than to live a boring life."

"And I'm sure that's exactly how you're going to wind up. I don't know you anymore, Brent. I truly don't recognize you at all," Brian said sadly.

Another loud shout from the street diverted Brent's attention. LeBarge was telling the men to search every room in the hotel.

"I gotta move," Brent said and headed for the door.

"No words for the family," Brian asked?

Brent thought for a second and then said, "Tell them I said Adios."

Brian stood there until Brent had opened the door and then said, "I'd wish you luck, but I'd be condoning your killing of some lawman somewhere."

"Save your preaching for Sunday School," Brent said and then stepped out into the hall.

Seeing the door that led to the outside staircase he hurried towards it. Brian moved into the doorway to watch his brother hurry off.

Just as Brent was nearing the door that led to the outside staircase it opened and two men entered. They both had their guns drawn. They stopped when they saw the tall man approaching them.

Brent never broke stride as he called out to them, "I've already checked the rooms on the right side of the hall. You boys check the ones on the left side. I'm on my way downstairs to check the four rooms down there."

The men looked at Brent and then nodded in agreement. Brent went passed them and when he reached the door stopped and looked back at Brian. He smiled and touched the brim of his hat before going through the doorway and down the stairs.

No sooner had Brian stepped back inside his room than there was several gunshots outside. Brian felt a knot in his stomach as he ran out the door and down the hall to the door to the outer stairs. He expected to see Brent lying dead at the bottom of the stairs. Instead there were two men from the makeshift posse lying on the ground.

It broke Brian's heart to think that his brother was the cause of this. He felt nauseated at the thought of Brent being on the run from the law. He knew that it was just a matter of time before Brent's luck ran out. Still, he said a silent prayer for the safety of his brother.

The two gunshots brought other members of the posse running to the hotel. Brent made it around the corner of the hotel and headed for the livery stable. As luck would have it a freighter was fixing to pullout from the freight office that was near the hotel and had gone back inside the office to pick up his manifest.

Brent saw his chance to get away and quickly slipped under the large canvas covering of the load. Now if some nosey lawman didn't raise the canvas to have a look see he'd be home free.

If the wagon was going in the direction of the livery stable Brent figured he'd slide off the back of the wagon when they neared it. If it went in the oopposit direction he'd wait until he was out of town and then knock the driver in the head and drive the team to the first place he could find and trade for a saddle horse.

The driver of the wagon returned shortly and climbed onto the wagon bench seat.

"Get up there, Red, Chigger, Blackie, Buck," the driver called out to his team of horses as he snapped the reins and the wagon moved out.

Brent's heart was beating fast and his senses were keen. He listened for any one ordering the wagon to stop so it could be inspected. He didn't know that several men had already checked it over shortly before he stowed away.

"I hope you catch that hombre, Zeke," the driver yelled to one of the deputies as he passed by him.

"We will, Tom, we've got this town sewn up tight."

Brent couldn't hold back a grin. So far things couldn't have gone along smoother. He just hoped his luck would hold a little bit longer.

The wagon was headed in the direction of the livery stable, Brent could tell that. He raised the canvas slightly so he could look out. He remembered a school house was near the stable and when he saw it he would know to get off the wagon. It wasn't long before they moved passed it.

Brent slid out of the back of the wagon without the driver ever knowing he had a stowaway aboard. Now if he could just get to his horse inside the livery stable. He figured that there would be a guard posted there, as well as the stagecoach office. He was right.

The man posted at the livery was an older gent. He had probably been given this job so he could sit down. The guard was armed with a double barrel shotgun, however. He wouldn't have to be much of a shot to make his shot count.

Brent walked up to the front door with a big smile on his face. The guard squinted into the night and called out, "Halt, who goes there?"

"Morgan," Brent said loudly. "Sheriff LeBarge sent me up here to relieve you. They think they have the guy cornered in the feed store. Roy said to have you come down there because of the shotgun. They need it since all the other men are armed with rifles and the bullets carry too far," Brent said, making things up as he went along.

"The feed store, eh. Yeah, I'll do that. I want to be there for the kill. I'll have something to tell my grandkids about...besides, I liked Murphy" the old gent said.

"Well, get a move on. They want to move in before he gets too comfortable in the store," Brent urged.

"Yeah, yeah, I don't want to miss this."

"Which one of these nags belongs to that jasper, anyway?"

"The good looking sorrel in the second stall," the old gent said.

Brent watched as the old man scurried down the street in the direction of town. He'd be long gone before the sheriff put two and two together. Hurriedly Brent bridled and saddled his horse. He wasted no time in mounting up and kicking the animal into a full gallop away from San Antonio.

Meanwhile, BJ had packed up his belongings and had left the hotel. He didn't want to take any chances on being in San Antonio when the smoke cleared on this mess. He decided against taking the time to see Selman's fiancé which was just as well. He'd send her a beautiful gift when he got back to Abilene. It was after two in the morning when he saddled up and headed out of San

Antonio. He wanted to be far away when the sun came up.

BJ's thoughts were on his brother and he hoped he'd gotten away without getting killed or hurting anyone. He thought of different ways of telling the family about his meeting up with Brent. Should he tell them the whole truth about him, or just that he was alive and didn't want to come home? He had a long ways to go in reaching Abilene, so he'd come up with something.

BJ had taken the trail north that would lead him through the small town of Medina, then up to another small settlement called Kerrville. He didn't know it at the time, but there was trouble waiting for him in both places.

Raymond D. Mason

5

ROYCE RAWLINGS **owned one of the biggest** ranches north of San Antonio. Royce was a hard man, but fair; his son Buster, however, was ruthless, hot tempered, and mean. Due to the Rawlings family's stature, they more or less ruled the town of Medina, and that included the local sheriff, Spud Winters.

Royce's daughter Barbara was a beauty with a sweet disposition, totally opposite of her brother, Buster. She had been schooled in the East for two years and was considered a lady by everyone who met her. She was Royce's pride and joy and never cast anything but a positive light on the family name.

"Buster, would you drive me into town so I can pick up a few things for the barbeque this weekend," Barbara asked her brother?

"Yeah, sure, Sis; I was going into town in a little while anyway. You'll have to drive yourself home, though. I'm going to stay in town for awhile," Buster replied and then added, "I want to see...uh, Marty."

"Marty..., don't you mean Florence. You know what Pa will do if he finds out you're still seeing her," Barbara warned.

"How's Pa going to know if you don't tell him," Buster said with a cocky grin on his face.

"I'm not going to tell him unless he asks me point blank. I'll not lie for you, Buster."

"Always the 'goody two shoes' aren't you, Sis. Well, I'll see who I want, when I want, and where I want, and no one, not even Pa, is going to tell me I can't do it. Pa may rule the ranch, but no one rules me," Buster growled.

"Buster, your attitude is going to get you in trouble one of these days. I'm afraid it'll be more trouble than Pa will be able to get you out of," Barbara said in a worried tone.

"I don't need Pa to get me out of trouble. That's why I carry two of these," Buster said, slapping his two pearl handled pistols.

"I'm afraid it's going to be those guns that get you into trouble. Them and your hot temper," Barbara said with a slight frown.

Barbara loved her brother, but hated his arrogance and hot temper. She had never seen the pure mean streak that ran through him, although she had heard rumors from those who had. She feared that Buster would run up against the wrong man one day and get himself killed.

Buster tied his horse to the back of the buckboard and the two of them headed into Medina. As they drove along they talked about the big barbeque they would be having that weekend. It was an annual event that everyone in the area looked forward to. It always found a couple of fist fights later in the day, after some of the working hands had downed a good amount of beer.

Brian reined his horse up in front of the Medina Saloon. He was tired, hot, and hungry and considered taking a room for the night in the only hotel in town. It was nearing high noon and he'd been in the saddle a good number of hours, having left San Antonio so early. First though, he wanted a cool beer to wash down the trail dust.

BJ counted six people in the saloon as he pushed open the batwing doors. Four men were playing cards and the lone bar girl stood near the poker table, watching the game. The bartender was wiping out a glass. When the woman saw BJ she smiled warmly and watched him as he walked up to the bar.

"Do you serve food in here," BJ asked the bartender when he reached the bar.

"If you buy a drink you can help yourself to the cold cuts and cheese down at the end of the bar," the bartender said with a slight grin.

"That'll do," BJ said, "Give me a beer."

The bartender drew a beer while BJ moved to the end of the bar containing the food. He made himself a good sized sandwich and when the bartender brought his glass of beer to him, tossed a quarter to the man.

"Beer's only a dime, I'll get your change," the bartender said.

"Keep it," BJ replied. "This sandwich is worth a lot more than fifteen cents to me."

Brian (BJ) took his beer and sandwich and walked over to a table and sat down. It wasn't long before the woman sidled over to where he was seated and smiled a seductive smile.

"Buy a working girl a drink," she asked?

"Why not...as long as it ain't champagne; I live on a beer budget," Brian said and chuckled.

"Don't most of us," the woman said. "Beer will do me just fine. You don't mind if I join you, do you?"

"No, not if you don't mind listening to growling noises that I make while eating this sandwich," BJ laughed.

"Mm, I like growling noises sometimes; if you get my meaning," the woman said coyly.

"I'll bet you do," BJ said and took another bite of his sandwich.

The woman looked over at the bartender and held up two fingers and then turned back towards Brian, "So where you headed?"

"Abilene," BJ replied.

"I was in Abilene once. It ain't much of a town," she said.

"Oh, and Medina is?"

She laughed, "You got me there. I guess Abilene is a sight bigger than Medina, huh."

"How's the hotel here in town? Is it safe," Brian asked?

"They've got a lock on the door; some of them actually work," the woman grinned, and then added. "But if it's a bed you're looking for...I have a big one right next door."

Brian grinned, "You come right to the point don't you. What's your name?"

"My full name is Florence, but my very close friends call me Flo...you can call me Flo...and you can call me anytime."

Brian chuckled, "I'd take you up on your offer, Flo, but I'm afraid I wouldn't get much rest."

"You wouldn't want any rest, tall man." Flo grinned.

"I'd need more rest. No, thanks, but right now I need rest. I've got a long road ahead of me and I've already traveled a long, long way," Brian said more serious

"If you change your mind, you know where to find me. I just want to make your stay here in Medina more memorable, that's all."

"I never took it any other way, Flo," Brian smiled again.

Flo was smiling when she looked from Brian to the batwings just as Buster entered. The smile dropped quickly from her face, causing Brian to follow her gaze. When he looked back at her he saw something in her eyes that he didn't like; fear. He looked back in the direction of the man who'd just entered and found him glaring in his and Flo's direction.

"A friend of yours," Brian asked?

"Uh huh...and trouble," Flo said as she moved her chair away from the table. "This man thinks he owns me."

Buster held his gaze on Flo and the stranger in town for several long seconds. Finally he moved in their direction, pulling his gloves off as he walked towards them. When he got within earshot of Flo he said with a sneer, "What'cha say, Flo? Who's this saddle bum you've taken up with?"

Brian felt an immediate dislike of the man.

Flo got up from her chair and rushed to Buster, "He's just a lonesome cowboy who's passing through Medina on his way to Abilene, that's all. How are you doing, honey?"

Buster looked around Flo and continued to glare at Brian. Not wanting any trouble, Brian turned his face away from Buster and drank down the last of his beer. He looked in the direction of the bar and motioned for the barkeep to draw him another beer.

"Are you just passing through our little town, saddle bum," Buster groused?

"If you're talking to me, big mouth, the answer is 'yes'. But let me warn you, you'd better not be talking to me," Brian said slow and evenly.

"Oh, the saddle bum is a tough guy. Are you a really bad man, saddle bum," Buster continued to prod.

"I think you've said enough, slick. You don't want to push your luck. Besides what business is it of yours where I'm going, or where I've been? I don't see that it's any of your business," Brian said in tight, clipped phrasing.

"Anything that goes on in Medina is my business. The Rawlings family runs this town and everyone in it. When I ask you a question, any question; you'd better answer up real quick like. Obviously you don't know who you're talking too," Buster snapped.

"I don't know and I don't care," Brian said evenly.

"You'll care when I knock a couple of your teeth out."

"You really scare me with your tough talk. Let me tell you something; bigger and better men than you have tried to do that, and I still have a full mouth of choppers."

Buster stood about five feet ten, while BJ stood a shade over six feet three. Seated the way he was, Buster didn't really know the size of the stranger he was talking too. It was only when BJ stood up that he realized how big he was. Buster quickly changed his bullying tactic by shifting his bravado to his guns.

"I'm the fastest man in these parts with these," Buster said slapping the grips of his pearl handled six shooters.

"Is that right," BJ said with a slight grin. "Then folks must be a might slow around here, because your reputation hasn't made it very far."

With Buster still glaring at him red faced, BJ turned his back on him and walked to the bar. When he reached it he said to the bartender, "Where's that beer, barkeep?" Then turning to look in Flo's direction asked, "Do you want another beer, Flo?"

"She ain't drinking with you, tramp; if she drinks it will be with me," Buster snapped angrily.

"I don't remember asking you about it, hot shot. I was talking to the lady."

Buster's neck was beet red by this time and his face flushed with anger. He struck a gunman's pose and glared at Sackett. BJ stood relaxed and poised. When he spoke his words came hard and sharp.

"If you go for those guns you'll die right here on this barroom floor. If you turn and walk out of here you'll live to bully someone else. The decision is yours to make; so make it."

Buster swallowed hard but his glare remained steady. No one had ever stood up to him this way before; not with ice cold confidence in their prowess with a gun. When Buster licked his lips BJ knew he was contemplating his chances of survival.

Just then a woman's voice from behind him broke the tension, "Buster will you help me load up the ... ," Barbara said as she entered the saloon, but cut her words short when she saw the situation that had developed.

"Get out of here, Sis," Buster called back to her never taking his eyes off of Brian.

"Your brother's got himself into a situation he doesn't know how to get out of, Ma'am," Brian said giving her a quick glance and then added, "If you want him to live longer you'd better get him out of here."

Barbara looked from Brian to Buster and then pleaded, "Please come with me, Buster; please."

Flo spoke up and added, "Listen to your sister, Buster. You've got a big weekend ahead of you; you don't want to dampen everyone's spirits with a shooting incident."

"The play is yours, hoss. Don't let your arrogant pride take you someplace you can't get out of," Brian said, his words clipped and tight.

"Think of all the fun folks are going to have at the barbeque, Buster. Think of your pa," Flo said again.

"Flo's right, Buster; Dad is so looking forward to this weekend. Don't do anything to ruin it for him and everyone else," Barbara pleaded.

Buster saw his way out the tight spot he'd worked himself into and decided to take it. He slowly moved his hands away from his guns and the tension in the room began to ease.

Giving the appearance of reluctance, Buster began to back slowly in the direction of the doorway. Barbara moved up and took Buster by the arm causing him to jerk it away from her grip violently.

"Come on Buster," Barbara coaxed as he reached the batwings.

"I'll see you again tramp, and next time will be different; of that you can be sure," Buster growled. Looking at Flo, he snapped, "I'll see you later, too!"

Just then Sheriff 'Spud' Winters walked through the doors but stopped when he saw Buster and Barbara standing there. Winters smiled, but it quickly faded when he saw the looks on Buster and Barbara's faces.

"What's going on here," Winters asked?

"I was just about to teach this no-account drifter a lesson," Buster said loudly, his bravado sneaking back into this behavior.

"Oh, is that right. Well maybe this is something I'd better handle, Buster," the sheriff said and then looked at BJ.

"Who are you, mister," the sheriff asked?

"You heard the loud mouth there, Sheriff; I'm just a no-account drifter," BJ answered.

"Don't sass me, boy. I'll ask you again...who are you?"

"Sackett is the name; from up Abilene way," BJ said with a disgusted look on his face.

"We don't cotton to strangers coming into town and causing trouble with our citizenry. Maybe you ought to be moving along," the sheriff said adjusting his gun belt.

"Sheriff, I came into town to have a bite to eat and rest up for the journey I have ahead of me. This man came in on the prod and started trying to pick a showdown with me. A showdown, I might add, that would have been his last," BJ said with a frown. "This young lady came in and saved his bacon and I'm all for that. Once I've picked up a few supplies I'll be moving on."

Casting a quick look at Barbara, Winters said quietly, "Get Buster out of here....now."

Buster gave BJ one last hard glare before moving past the sheriff and going outside with his sister. Winters waited until they had gone and then he turned back towards BJ.

"I want you out of town by sundown. If I see you here after that, I'll lock you up. Any business you have, you take care of it and then hit the leather," the sheriff said.

"You might try asking some of these men in the saloon what happened here. I'm sure there's at least one honest man among them that will tell you the truth," BJ said tightly.

"I don't care what anyone here says; I told you the way it's going to be. Now, you do it," Winters snapped harshly.

"Buster is one of the county's richest men, mister," one of the patrons who had seen everything said.

"Oh, I thought that might be the case. I know the type," Brian replied, and then added, "I take it you're on the old man's payroll, is that right sheriff," Brian asked.

Winters bristled, "I ain't on anyone's payroll. I serve the good people of Medina and that's all. And what's more, I'll not have some stranger in town accuse me of any wrong doing."

The sheriff whirled around and stormed out of the saloon. Once he was gone the bartender said quietly to BJ, "You hit the nail right smack dab on the head. It did my heart good to see someone put that blowhard Buster on the run. You put a scare into him and I loved what you just said to the sheriff. He is on the Rawlings payroll. Be careful though, cowboy, don't push them too hard."

Barbara drove the wagon back to the ranch, relieved that Buster had not killed the stranger, or that the stranger hadn't killed Buster. Now that the tenseness was a thing of the pass, Barbie was able to concentrate her thoughts on the way the stranger looked. A smile came to her face as she thought to herself, 'what a good looking man the stranger is.'

49

Brian decided to pick up his supplies and then head on out of Medina and rest up at the first place along the trail where he could make camp. He didn't know that where he decided to pitch camp would lead to his saving Royce Rawlings; Buster Rawlings' father's, life.

As Barbie began unloading the supplies she bought in town out of the wagon, Judd Hoover rounded the corner of the house. When he saw Barbie holding a large box of supplies he rushed over to give her a hand.

"Let me help you with that, Miss Rawlings," Hoover said.

"Oh, thank you Judd; it is a little heavy. Let me get one of the smaller boxes and then follow me into the kitchen," Barbie said with a smile.

She picked up one of the lighter boxes and walked up alongside Hoover. As they started for the kitchen Barbie looked up at the ranch foreman and asked, "Judd, why do you always call me 'Miss Rawlings' instead of calling me Barbie, or even Barbara?"

"Why, because you're the bosses daughter and it wouldn't be right for me, one of the ranch hands, to call you anything but Miss Rawlings," Judd replied truthfully.

"You know I don't mind if you call me by my first name; and I know father wouldn't mind either. I refer to you by your first name," Barbie stated.

"I just wouldn't feel right doing it ma'am. I guess it's just my upbringing," Judd said with a slight grin.

"Well, if you ever change your mind, just remember it won't bother me in the least," Barbie offered.

They set the boxes down on the large kitchen table and then Judd started to go back for the other boxes when Miss Rawlings stopped him.

"You wouldn't happen to know where father is, would you, Judd?"

"He said he was going to ride out to the north range and check on the cattle. They've been getting bogged down in that black mud hole. We've lost three head of cattle in that stuff over the last month," Judd answered.

"I hope he's all right. You know how he pushes himself," Barbie said with a worried look on her face.

"He should be back in an hour or so. Do you want me to ride out and check on him," Judd asked?

"No, I don't want to make him feel like I don't trust him to take care of himself. You know how independent he is. If he's not back in an hour, though, I might ask you to do so."

"You just say the word, Miss Rawlings," Judd said with a grin.

Buster Rawlings leered at the new hire that August Dorchester had working for him. August looked at young Rawlings and rolled the long black cigarillo from one side of his mouth to the other.

"So what do you think, Buster? Think she'll pass muster," August asked with a grin?

"She'll do me just fine," Buster replied and then turned his attention from the girl to August, "How much," he asked pointedly?

"Hey for you...it'll only be five dollars the first time. It'll be ten dollars from then on," August said proudly.

Buster looked at August and then back at the woman, "Well, I'll have to see what I'm buying. I don't buy anything sight unseen, August, you know that, don't you."

"I wouldn't expect you too, Buster," August said and then glared at the woman, "Strip off them clothes and let Mr. Rawlings get a good look at you."

The woman stood with her eyes downcast and her head hanging low. This was humiliating for the young woman and Buster could see it. Not being the gentleman his father had hoped he would be, he saw her humility as a weakness.

"Put this on my account," Buster said and reached for the woman's arm. When she pulled away, he bristled, "Come on woman, don't you pull back from me. I'll give you something to pull back from."

"Hey, no rough stuff, Buster. You remember what I said after the rough stuff with Polly. I'll bar you from ever coming in here and I think your papa would back me up on my action."

Buster's eyes narrowed, "I'll settle up with you at the barbeque we're having this weekend. Pa's always in a good mood during the barbecue. Besides, that it's payday and he pays me on the same day he pays the rest of the ranch hands. I've never stiffed anyone out of money yet, and I ain't starting to now, especially you, August. You've got the girls."

"Just remember, Buster, when you don't pay me, the girls don't get paid and I've got to keep them happy or they'll head for San Antone, or some other big city," August went on.

Buster wanted to get up to the room with the new gal and August was keeping him from his pleasure. He knew what would shut the man up, money.

"I'll tell you what I'll do, August, I'll not only give you what I owe you at the barbeque, but I'll give you a little extra for your trouble; how's that," Buster asked?

August's grin spread from one ear to the other. Buster was his best customer, visiting his place at least once a week, but seemed to enjoy making a game out of holding back the money he owed.

Buster took the new girl by the hand and started up the stairs. Ruby, one of August's other girls whispered to the girl seated next to her, "Well, I guess that means he won't want to see me anymore."

"Yeah, and you was his favorite. Maybe he won't like Betty," the second gal replied.

"I wasn't complaining about him not seeing me anymore. I'm thankful for it. He could get down right mean and hurtful."

"Oh, I was always a little bit jealous because he always wanted to bed you. You never let on that you didn't like him."

"I liked his money, honey. Every time he got too rough he'd always leave a little extra something on the table. I might miss the money, but I sure won't miss Buster. Besides that, now I feel free to go after Buster's old man when he comes in here. I hear he leaves a sight more of a tip than Buster ever did...and he ain't crazy."

Raymond D. Mason

6

BRIAN SACKETT heard the refreshing sound of rippling water before he ever saw the wide stream. He was ready for a peaceful rest since he had not gotten any sleep the night before. This looked and sounded like the ideal spot to make camp.

He stepped down off his horse and raised his horse's right front leg. Sure enough, he thought the horse favored that leg slightly. It was missing the horseshoe. He'd have to find a blacksmith in the next town to have one put on.

While he was in the process of loosening the cinch on the saddle he heard what he thought might be a faint cry for help. He listened intently wanting to make sure it wasn't just the wind whispering through the grove of cottonwoods. He heard the sound again and knew it was a man calling for help.

BJ waded across the stream in the direction of the sound of the man's voice. When he rounded a small thicket he heard the cry again and moved on in that direction. Just over the edge of the stream bank he saw the top half of a saddled horse. As he moved slowly towards the horse he saw its rider, also.

The man had fallen off the horse and was lying on his back with his foot caught in the stirrup. He was lying in the water and the horse looked as though it were about to bolt. Brian knew he would have to be very careful in approaching the animal.

"Lay very still," Brian said just loud enough for the man to hear him. I'll get my horse and ride over to you."

Moving very cautiously Brian moved back in the direction of his horse and once out of sight of the downed rider and horse, he moved faster. Mounting up he rode back across the stream and made his way to where the man was lying.

The big sorrel the man had been riding stood motionless except for pricking up its ears as BJ moved his mount up alongside it. Brian reached over slowly and took hold of the reins. Once he had a good grip on them he stepped down off his horse and moved around to the side where the man was laying.

Brian worked the man's boot out of the stirrup which had gotten caught when he fell from the saddle. The reason was the short heel on the boots the man was wearing.

"I'd advise you against wearing these walking heel boots when you go for a ride," BJ said evenly.

"Danged heel almost got me killed," the man said as he got to his feet. "I want to thank you, young man, for coming along when you did and responding to my call for help."

"Don't mention it. You can actually thank a young tough in Medina for me being here at this precise time. If it hadn't been for being told to leave town by the local sheriff I'd be sacked out in a hotel room about now," BJ grinned.

"Oh; and why were you asked to leave town," the man asked?

"Just a little run in with one of the locals; no harm done to anyone," BJ replied.

"Well, whatever the reason was I just thank God that it happened the way it did. If that horse would have bolted he'd have dragged me to death," the man said and then added, "Where are you headed, anyway?"

"Abilene...the one in Texas, not Kansas," BJ laughed.

"You've got a long ride ahead of you. It looks to me like you've been in the saddle quite awhile already. How would you like to put up at my ranch for awhile," the man said sincerely?

Brian thought for a second before answering and then said, "You know, that sounds good to me. I just noticed that my horse is missing a shoe so I could put one on there. Yeah, I'll take you up on your offer; thank you."

"Good, that settles it. Now if I can just manage to stay aboard this blasted brush jumper we'll head for the ranch," the man said with a chuckle and then added. "By the way, son, my name is Royce Rawlings. What might yours be?"

"My friends call me BJ, that's short for Brian Joseph," BJ said.

"Mind if I call you BJ?"

"Not at all; I'd say we're friends, wouldn't you," BJ chuckled.

The two men headed off at an easy gallop in the direction of the Double R Ranch; the Royce Rawlings brand.

"That does it Buster, I want you out of here now," August Dorchester yelled as he held the young woman Buster had been with against his chest; her nose bleeding from the punch administered by Buster.

"What kind of a place are you running here, August? I caught this little tramp going through my pants pockets," Buster snapped angrily.

"I wasn't, August, honest I wasn't. His pants had fallen off the chair where he had laid them and I was just putting them back when he woke up. I wasn't going through his pockets," the girl sobbed.

"Are you missing anything, Buster? Have you even checked," August asked angrily?

"I don't have to check; I know what I saw," Buster said instinctively reaching for the pocket he carried his money clip in.

"Well, you might look and see if anything is missing before you go hittin' on the girl," August said and patted the girl's shoulder. "Don't cry honey, I believe you."

Buster pulled his money clip out and checked his bills. He still had every dollar he had come in with. He took on an arrogant look and attitude.

"Maybe I'll have to take my business else where. It ain't that far into San Antonio, and I hear that there's a new house opening up in Kerrville," Buster paused before adding, "I guess you don't want me to settle up for what I owe you, is that right?"

"Oh, you'll settle up all right. I'll have a little chat with your pa. You know how much he hates people who don't pay up what they owe. He'll see that I get what's coming to me," August answered. "I also know how he feels about men who beat up women. I think you do too, don't you Buster?"

Buster knew that his father and August had been friends for a long time and there was no way his pa would let him cheat August out of his money. He also knew that his pa hated women beaters with a passion.

Buster turned and stormed towards the front door. One of the girls called after him, "You all come back now, hear?"

Three Days to Sundown

Buster rode his horse hard, all the way to the ranch. When he arrived the horse was covered with lather. As he rode up to the corral, Judd Hoover, the foreman, walked out of the barn. When he saw the condition of the horse he bristled.

"Are you trying to kill that horse, Buster?

"I was in a hurry."

"I don't care if the entire Kiowa nation was after you; you don't run a horse like that," Hoover snapped.

"I'll ride my horse anyway I want to, and no common cowhand is going to tell me different," Buster cracked back.

"Would you say the same thing to your pa if he were here?"

"Well, I don't see Pa around here anywhere; do you Hoover?"

Judd looked at the young Rawlings and slowly shook his head, "Someday, Buster, you're going to run up against the wrong man and he's going to kill you."

"Oh, you think so, do you? Well, he'll have to be a better man than you, Judd."

"Take those guns off and say that. There's no one around and we'll just see who the better man is with their fists," Judd said with a frown.

"I play for keeps. If you want a piece of me...go for that gun on your hip."

"I'm not a gunman, and neither are you. It takes more than a quick draw to make someone a gunfighter, Buster. One day you'll learn that."

"Talk, talk, talk; that's all I hear from you, Judd," Buster sneered.

"You'd better hope your pa never fires me, squirt. The last thing I'll do before leaving this ranch is beat you to within an inch of your life," Judd said seriously, meaning every word.

Buster glared hard at Judd, but didn't have a comeback remark. He knew he was close to pushing the foreman too far. He'd seen Judd handle some unruly men that had been fired and he wanted no part of any fisticuffs with Hoover.

"Where's Pa," he asked, changing the subject.

"I don't know. I thought he was over at the black water pool, but one of the men came in from that area and said he hadn't seen him. He should be coming back shortly though," Judd said, his temper cooling down a bit.

Just then Barbie walked out the front door and when she saw the two men talking, trotted across to where they were.

"Has father returned yet, Judd," Barbie asked?

"No, not yet, Miss Rawlings; do you want me to go and look for him," Judd asked?

"Maybe you ought to; I worry about him being out on the range alone," she said.

"My god, Barbie; the old man's all right; you treat him like he's helpless. He'll live to be two hundred years old with my luck," Buster said angrily.

"With your luck, did you say? In other words you would like to see father dead, Buster? That's a terrible thing to say," Barbie said in a shocked tone.

"I didn't mean it that way. I just wish he'd give me more of a voice in the running of the ranch, that's all. He gives Hoover here more power than he does me," Buster complained.

"Judd earned it," Barbie said evenly.

"Oh, and I haven't, is that what you're saying?"

"I'm just saying that Judd has more experience at running a ranch than you do. You've been to busy chasing after the ladies in the county," Barbie said with a wry smile.

Just hen the sound of hoof beats caused the three of them to look in the direction of the barn. Rounding the corner was Royce and Brian. They rode up to where the three were standing. When Buster saw who was with his father, his eyes widened noticeably.

Brian recognized both Buster and Barbie and frowned slightly. Barbie's mouth opened as she started to say something, but didn't.

"What're you doing with this guy," Buster asked?

"This guy, as you call him, saved my life. This is BJ, Brian Joseph; Brian this is my son Buster, and my daughter, Barbie, and Judd Hoover, my foreman."

"We've all ready met," Buster snapped.

"Oh, is that right. Where'd you meet at," Royce Rawlings asked his son, but looked towards Brian?

"In town," Buster said, spitting the words out.

Royce grinned slightly as he continued to look at Brian and asked the question, "The young tough?"

Brian nodded slowly, "The young tough."

Royce looked back at his son and snapped angrily, "What have I told you about going on the prod, Buster. I've warned you about your bullying antics and I'm telling you again. Straighten up or I'll take those guns away from you and give 'em to someone who has the right character to own 'em. Now apologize to this young man."

"You don't even know what it was over, Pa. You're taking a complete stranger's word on something that happened between us over your own son's,' Buster complained?

"I know my own son, and I know that this young man saved my life. If he hadn't happened along when he did I'd probably be dead by now," Royce said, his words firm.

"Oh no, Father, what happened," Barbie asked quickly?

"Oh, it was my own fault. I wore these blasted walking heeled boots instead of the boots with the riding heel and fell off Molly. My foot got caught in the stirrup and if Mr. Joseph hadn't come along, I'd be dead by now, I'm sure."

Brian grinned, "My last name isn't Joseph, sir. Joseph is my middle name."

"Oh, I'm sorry...that's what the BJ is for," Royce said with a grin. "What is your last name, then?"

"Sackett," BJ said.

"Sackett," Royce exclaimed, "Sackett from Abilene? You wouldn't be related to a John Sackett by any chance would you," Royce asked curiously?

"He's my dad. Have you heard of him?'

"Heard of him...hell, boy, we're old friends. We used to punch cattle together before we went our separate ways. I wondered what had happened to him. Oh, I've seen the name Sackett around, and even wondered if it was the John Sackett I knew," Royce said excitedly.

"Wait a minute...did you and my pa court the same young lady for awhile," Brian asked?

"We sure did. It's a good thing we were the best of pals or we'd have come to blows over that little filly," Royce laughed.

"That's the one who ran off with the whiskey drummer who came through town, right," Brian said with a grin?

"That's the one all right. Well, I'll be hanged for a horse thief...John Sackett's son right here on my ranch. This is a pleasant surprise. You know your pa saved my bacon once too. Maybe he's told you about it."

"D'you mean with the Comanche's chasing you and your horse fell?"

"That's it. John came riding back and I swung up behind him and we made it to Fort Blaine just ahead of them red sticks. Yep, he sure saved my bacon all right," Royce said thoughtfully. "And now his son saves me from my own horse," he said and let out with a loud laugh that made the others laugh as well; all but Buster, that is.

Buster waited until they'd all had their laugh and then asked, "How long are you going to let this guy stay here?"

"As long as he wants to, Buster; do you have a problem with that," Royce asked with a frown?

Buster cast a hard look at Brian, "No, I guess not; as long as he gives me plenty of room."

"You don't have to worry about that, hoss. I didn't come looking for trouble," Brian replied and then looked at Judd Hoover. "Do you have a spare bunk in the bunkhouse," he asked?

"It just so happens we do...Mr. Sackett."

"You can call me BJ. Mr. Sackett is my father," BJ said getting a grin from Hoover.

"Well, I'll let you get squared away and then I want you to come up to the big house and fill me in on everything your pa has been up to," Royce said with a big smile. "Of course, you and Judd will have dinner with us."

Buster shook his head slowly as he turned and walked away. Royce watched his son depart and then turned his attention to BJ. "I hope you'll forgive my boy for his rudeness, Brian. He's sure got a lot of foolish pride in him."

"I'll avoid him as much as possible. I'll only be here long enough to rest up and put that shoe on my horse. Then I'll be heading home," Brian said.

"I hope you'll wait until after the big barbeque we have planned for this weekend. It's always good and this year's going to be a doozy," Royce said with a grin.

"Yes it would be nice if you could stay," Barbie agreed.

Brian looked at her and smiled. He had noticed her good looks at their first meeting in town, but now he saw that she was a beautiful woman. And it was obvious that she was nothing like her brother.

"Okay, I'll stay until after the barbeque. It does sound like everyone has a good time. Thank you for the offer," Brian said.

"**What; do you mean to tell me that Pa asked** that no account to stay for the party," Buster ranted when Barbie broke the news to him.

"Buster...his father and ours were the best of friends when they were younger. It's only right that we should invite him to stay for the barbeque. Why do you always have to wear that chip on your shoulder? Just once I wish you'd try to behave when something doesn't go exactly how you want it," Barbie scolded.

"That's easy for you to say; you're Miss Perfect. You couldn't do anything wrong in the old man's eyes if you tried. Everyone knows you're his favorite over me," Buster complained.

"You know that's only because I remind him of mother. He misses her terribly."

"She's been gone over three years now. He couldn't miss her all that much; he still makes an occasional trip to August's," Buster answered back.

"You would mention that. I guess he still has urges like any man," Barbie said taking her father's side.

"Well, I still don't think he should have invited this Sackett guy to stay. He'd better stay away from me if he knows what's good for him self."

"Promise me you won't start any trouble with him...besides, I think he's quite handsome," Barbie said truthfully.

"Handsome...you probably think Judd Hoover is handsome too."

"Actually, I do; in a rugged sort of way."

"Let's face it, Sis. You're looking for a man. How old are you now, twenty two?"

"So what does that have to do with anything?"

"You're probably afraid of becoming an old maid."

"Not hardly Buster...I'll know the right man when he comes along. And for your information Brian Sackett could just be that man. What do you think about that?"

"For your sake I hope he isn't, because if I was around him very long I'm afraid you'd become a widow."

"You're impossible to carry on a decent conversation with, Buster. I have to go down and help with dinner," Barbie said and walked out of Buster's room.

Brian had laid down on the empty bunk and gone right off to sleep. He was dog-tired from his long night and half a day without sleep. Judd Hoover woke him up at around five thirty with a gentle nudge.

"Wake up, Sackett. We're invited up to the big house for dinner. They said for us to come up around a quarter to six. Better get a move on."

Brian sat up and rubbed his eyes. They felt like they had small grains of sand in them; indicating he had not gotten all the sleep he needed. Still, he got up and walked over to a small table that had a wash basin and a pitcher of water on it and splashed a handful of water in his face.

The other wranglers had began coming in from the different parts of the ranch. Several of them had already inquired of Hoover about the new man. Hoover had explained to them that he was just passing through and had saved Royce's life.

One of the wranglers grinned at Brian and said, "I hear you rescued Mr. Rawlings from a bad accident."

"It could have been. I'll bet he'll never take off on horseback wearing a low heeled boot again," Brian replied.

"Nothing he does surprises me," the man said.

Brian looked at him and wondered what the man had based that comment on. Judd grinned slightly and nodded his head in agreement. When he saw Brian looking at him, he explained.

"Royce suffered a hard fall a year after his wife passed away and we've noticed him doing a few odd things ever since. He managed to get lost on his own ranch a couple of times in the last six months. It's almost like he gets disoriented and goes in the opposite direction from which he wants to go. It could be that he's just getting a little older I guess," Hoover said.

"He may have suffered a more serious head injury than first realized," Brian said.

"That's a definite possibility."

Judd paused for a moment, "If you don't mind my asking, what was the trouble between you and Buster over?"

"I don't mind. It was really over a woman named Flo sitting at my table when Buster walked into the saloon. He didn't like her sitting with a 'saddle tramp'. I'm glad his sister was in town with him. It was actually her appearing there that broke the tension that had built to a boiling point," Brian said.

"I figured it was something like that. He's tangled with a few of the local cowboys over her. They haven't stood up to him because of the sheriff's allegiance to him. The two of them are pretty close and it would be tough on anyone who roughed Buster up. One day, though," Hoover said shaking his head.

"If he pushed the wrong man he's liable to have to prove just how handy he is with those guns he wears," Brian added.

"D'you mean the ones that Royce threatened to take away from Buster," Judd said with a chuckle?

BJ grinned, "That's the ones."

"I think this just might be the best barbeque we've ever had on this ranch. I wouldn't want to miss a minute of it, I can tell you that," Judd said getting agreeing nods from all the other ranch hands that had came in.

7

BLACK JACK HAGGERTY sat by the front window in the Sundown Saloon and Dance Hall, and watched the comings and going of people in the Sundown Cattlemen's Bank across the street. He was waiting for Frank Jordan to come back from having a tooth pulled at the local dentist office.

He had done this every day when he and Frank Jordan had come into town. He was laying out a plan for robbing the bank the day he and Jordan decided to move on. This day, however, would prove to be a little more informative and cause him to rethink what he had laid out so far.

Haggerty and Jordan had been staying at a cousin's place for a week and he'd promised the man that he wouldn't do anything to cause trouble. He figured he could come up with a plan that would leave his cousin in the clear, and even he wouldn't know for sure who had robbed the bank.

Jordan crossed the street holding his jaw. The dentist's office was three doors down from the bank so Haggerty had spotted his friend as soon as he had exited the dentist's office. Walking through the batwing doors

Jordan looked around for his friend and when he saw him walked quickly to his table.

"So how was it," Haggerty asked?

"It wasn't all that bad. He uses laughing gas and," he chuckled, "I'm still seeing everything as funny." Again he laughed.

Haggerty couldn't hold back a smile seeing as how he hadn't heard Jordan laugh all that many times.

"Wait until that stuff wears off; you might be singing a different tune," Haggerty stated.

"So what did you notice about the bank today," Jordan asked, changing the subject?

"Same as before; the busiest times of the day are when the bank first opens and then again around twelve-Noon," Haggerty said.

Jordan took on a ponderous look; when Haggerty noticed he asked about it.

"What is it, Frank?"

"It's something I overheard while in the dentist's office. He had just finished giving me that laughing gas and I was woozy. I could have sworn I heard the dentist talking to another man about a large deposit coming to the bank. It had something to do with two different cattle drives by some local ranchers."

Haggerty's eyes widened, "When; did they say?"

"I can't remember off hand. They may have, but everything is fuzzy," Jordan said shaking his head.

"Frank, you've got to remember when these deposits are going to be made. This could be really big," Haggerty urged.

"I know, I know; I'm trying to recall. Give me a little time and maybe I can recollect what they said."

"While you're trying to recall, I'll ask around and see if anyone else might know about it. Obviously the man you heard tell it to the dentist would know. Was the man a patient?"

"I don't know, Jack. He may have been. Wait a minute; no he wasn't because he came to the door of the room where the dentist does his work. No, he must have just been a friend of the dentist," Jordan said snapping his finger.

"I saw the owner of the general store go into the bank, and then went over to the dentist's office. He seemed like he was in a hurry. Then he come out about ten minutes later. He must have been the one you heard talking to the dentist," Haggerty said as he thought back. He then added, "Come on, Frank, let's do a little snooping around the general store and see what we might overhear."

"I'd like to have a drink of whiskey first. I'm afraid this laughing gas is starting to wear off."

"Go ahead and have your drink. You can come over to the general store when you're finished," Haggerty said as he got up to go.

"Okay, I'll be over there shortly," Jordan said and then noticed a poker game going on in the rear of the saloon. "When we finish in the general store maybe I'll sit in on that poker game. The gas should be totally worn off by then," Jordan said more to himself than to Haggerty.

"If you want to just go ahead and get in it now. I'll check out the general store. Besides, two of us in there at the same time might stir up a little suspicion, Frank. Go ahead and get in the game; that'll look better," Haggerty said with another angle in mind.

His thought was that he just might find out something that would give him an edge over Jordan where the money was concerned. He had no qualms about holding money back on the split. If Frank wasn't interested enough to go with him, then he shouldn't get an equal share of the take.

Haggerty walked across the street to the general store and began to browse around. When the owner's wife asked if she could help him find what he was looking for, he told her he was looking for a present for a friend of his, but didn't really know what he wanted. He figured that when he saw it he would then know.

Haggerty moved over near a couple of women who were looking at some new hat arrivals. They were chatting about everything, but when Haggerty overheard one of them say she'd be glad when her husband came back off the cattle drive, his ears perked up.

"I didn't think I'd miss him as much as I have," she said with a chuckle. "I guess I care a lot more about him than I knew."

The other woman laughed, "Oh, Kate, you always say that and everyone knows you're crazy about Bill. When are you expecting him back," her friend asked?

"In about a week. He's coming back with Mr. Chalmers. I've got plans for that bonus he was promised. It should be a good one; they got five dollars a steer more than they'd planned on. Mrs. Chalmers will be buying a few new clothes, you can bet on that."

"How much did they get for the cattle," the other woman asked?

"Bill's wire didn't say, but when they left they were hoping to get thirty dollars a head. I guess they got thirty five a head," the woman named Kate said.

"Oh, Kate; you said they were driving more than three thousand head to the rail head when Bill left. Let's see thirty five times three thousand would be...," she paused while she figured the numbers in her head.

Before she had the amount figured up, Kate said, "One hundred and five thousand dollars."

"Oh, my goodness; what we could do with that kind of money...I hate to think."

"The only way we will ever see that kind of money is if we rob a bank," Kate said and the two women broke out in laughter.

Haggerty had all the information he needed. One hundred and five thousand dollars from just one of the ranchers who had taken cattle to market. This could be the biggest bank job they had ever pulled, by far. Now he had an amount to deal with; too bad Jordan wasn't here to hear that amount.

When he got back to the saloon he found Jordan sitting in the poker game. He walked back and sat down at the empty table next to the card players. When one of the saloon girls walked up he told her he wanted a beer. She nodded okay and went back to the bar to fetch it.

Jordan looked over at Haggerty's table and said, "Did you find out what it was you wanted to know?"

"Yeah, I sure did. I'll have to tell you all about it sometime," Haggerty said with a slight frown.

"I'll be here for awhile. Maybe you'd like to wait upstairs in one of the rooms," Jordan said with a wry grin.

Haggerty looked at the stack of chips in front of Jordan and could see that he was several hundred dollars ahead. That was good because they were beginning to run a little low on funds.

"I might take you up on that. Of course, I'd have to borrow some money from you," Haggerty replied.

"Here," Jordan said and tossed him five, ten dollar chips.

Haggerty got up and walked to where the saloon gal was just getting his beer.

"I'll take that, honey," Haggerty said as he walked up behind her. He then added, "You wouldn't know a gal that would be willing to show a cowboy a good time would you?"

The woman looked him up and down before answering, "It all depends on what was in it for her."

"Oh, I thought it might depend on who was in her," Haggerty joked.

The woman gave a polite chuckle, "Cute, real cute."

"I'd say it might be worth ten dollars, maybe fifteen...if she was real good," Haggerty said, giving her the once over.

The woman looked at the bartender, "Joe, I'm going to take a break," she said.

"How long will you be gone, Carla," the bartender asked?

"That all depends on this gentleman."

"I'd say at least an hour," Haggerty said.

"Oh, a full hour, eh," the bartender replied and then added, "Looks like you've got a real admirer there, Carla."

Haggerty frowned at the bartender and lowered his voice, "What did you mean by that crack?"

The bartender looked at Haggerty's furrowed brow and knew he'd crossed an invisible line with this guy.

"I didn't mean anything by it. I just meant that usually the men can only afford about thirty minutes," the bartender stated.

"Oh...well, that's not so bad," Haggerty said as he relaxed slightly. "Come on, honey; let's get this party started."

"I have to warn you, that I'll have to come back down here at four o'clock. The bank president always comes over for a quick Brandy before he goes home and he always asks me to join him. He's a regular and I don't want to disappoint him. We'll have plenty of time together though, seeing as how it's only a little after two," Carla warned.

"Oh, that's fine, just fine. In fact, if the bank president doesn't mind I'd like to buy you and him both a Brandy," Haggerty said with a wide smile.

"I'm sure he won't mind and you know I won't mind. I think we're going to get along just wonderfully, bug boy," Carla laughed.

At five minutes to four the bank president walked through the saloon doors and looked around the room until he spotted Carla. He headed her way, but slowed when he noticed the man seated next to her.

Walking up to the table where Carla and Haggerty was, the bank president said, "I hoped you would have a Brandy with me, Carla."

"Oh, I am Harvey; I was just talking with this gentleman and he offered to buy us both a Brandy," Carla said gaily.

"Well, that's awfully nice of you, sir. I don't believe I've seen you around town before. I'm Harvey Abercrombie, and I'm the president of the bank over there. What is your name, if you don't mind my asking?"

"No I don't mind. It's Bill Smith; it's nice to make your acquaintance. I know you are a Brandy man, so I ordered us a bottle," Haggerty said in a friendly tone.

"Oh, usually I only have one Brandy and talk to Carla, here. Then I go home for dinner with my wife," Abercrombie said apologetically.

"Well, you usually don't come in until about ten minutes after four, Harvey," Carla smiled. "You're a little early today."

"Oh, so I am. Well, maybe one more Brandy wouldn't hurt. I really had a busy day and I need the Brandy to help me relax," Harvey said.

"A lot of business, huh," Haggerty asked nonchalantly.

"Yes and it's going to get busier tomorrow," Harvey went on.

"Oh, why's that," Haggerty pressed?

"We've got a ..., oh, I can't really talk about it. It's highly confidential. Let me just say that I'm going to be extra busy tomorrow," Harvey went on.

"The banking business must be a demanding job, I'd think," Haggerty said, appearing to change the subject.

"You'll never know unless you've been in the banking business yourself," the president said closing his eyes.

"I'm kind of in the banking business. Well, I should say, I do a lot of business with banks. I'm an investor and I'm in and out of banks on a regular basis," Haggerty said easily.

"Oh, an investor, eh; uh, what are you looking at around here, if you don't mind my asking," Harvey asked?

"No, I don't mind at all; it's cattle. I invest in cattle. You see we have a large ranch up in Montana and I go around and check out good stock for breeding purposes. My associate and I are always interested in business ventures of any kind, however," Haggerty lied.

"That is interesting. I'll have to tell some of my depositors about you. We have several large ranchers who are always on the look out for investment opportunities. Maybe I could set up a meeting between you and them and you could go over some of your investment opportunities with them. I know several that will have large sums of cash to invest," Harvey said as he poured himself another Brandy.

"I'd be more than happy to meet with them. My business associate and I will be leaving town very shortly, however; I'd have to meet with them in the next few days. We have a meeting out in California next month, so we'll be catching a train out that way," Haggerty said continuing the lie.

"Both parties I'm thinking of will be returning either tomorrow or the next day. I'll talk to them as soon as they get back and I will be the first person they see when they reach town. I can set up a meeting for a night that meets with everyone's approval," Harvey planned?

"That sounds perfect for us. I'll tell my associate and we'll be ready to move quickly on anything we can come to terms on. I want to thank you for this Mr. Abercrombie.

It is really big of you to do this for us," Haggerty said smoothly.

"No, no, I need to thank you, Mr. Smith. We don't get too many chances to invest in anything around here, other than local businesses that are going in. And, as you can see there's not a lot of growth taking place around Sundown. These men will be very interested in what you have to say, I'm sure."

"Have another Brandy, Mr. Abercrombie. You can't walk on one leg," Haggerty said happily.

"Oh, I've had one all ready...or was it two?"

"Who's counting, that's what I always say," Haggerty laughed, drawing a titter from Harvey as well.

Carla had been very quiet, merely listening to the conversation. She was beginning to get suspicious about the way Haggerty had been talking. He had said nothing to her about any of what he was saying to Mr. Abercrombie. She had the feeling something was up.

Always looking for an opportunity herself, she felt she might have stumbled onto a way of making some money out of what was going on. If this Bill Smith was on the up and up, she might invest in his venture. But, if he was planning on robbing the bank, she wanted in on that as well. She'd have to play her cards just right. And she knew just how to do it.

Brent Sackett sat astraddle his horse with one leg thrown casually over the saddle horn. He rolled himself a cigarette as he watched the stagecoach road below him. He had rolled a couple of good sized rocks into the road in such a way that the stagecoach could not get around them. The driver and guard would have to get down off the stagecoach to roll the rocks out of the way.

Brent had smoked about half of the cigarette when he spotted the stagecoach round a far off bend. He quickly climbed down off his horse and moved to a spot that was only about ten feet from one of the rocks in the road, but still well concealed. Now all he had to do was to wait; and he didn't have to wait long.

The stagecoach rounded the bend that was about one hundred yards from the boulders. Brent could hear the horses begin to slow down. Brent was about to rob his first stagecoach.

The coach pulled to a squeaking halt with both the guard and the driver scouring the countryside for any sign of holdup men or Indians. After feeling quite sure there were neither in the immediate area, the driver climbed down off his perch.

"Keep an eye out for anything suspicious, Corky," the driver warned.

"Don't worry, Red, I've got both hammer jacked back on this double barrel. You just roll those rocks out or the way," the guard said.

"You're going to have to give me a hand; either you or one of the passengers," the driver called back.

"I'll get one of the passengers."

While the guard was trying to get one of the passengers to lend a hand, the driver was moving up to where the larger rock was placed. As he started to move the boulder, Brent whispered, "Don't make a move or you're a dead man."

The driver froze, casting a quick look at the man wearing the bandana over his nose and covering half of his face.

"Do as you're told and no body will get hurt. Don't obey my every command and I will kill each and every passenger...after I drop the hammer on you," Brent said evenly.

"You've got my full attention, mister," the driver said.

"Call the guard over here to help you."

"Hey, Corky, give me a hand with this. It's too big for me to move by myself."

"I've got the biggest one of our passengers to help us. Come on Mr. Rubio, you can give us a hand," Corky said.

"Hurry up, Corky," Red urged.

"Hold your horses, Red. We'll be there in a second," Corky yelled back somewhat perturbed.

"You just go ahead like you're trying to move that rock. Remember, the first one to get it if anything goes wrong will be you," Brent whispered.

Corky leaned the shotgun against a rock that was just off the road, and he and Mr. Rubio made their way over to give Red a hand. When they got there and started to roll one of the rocks out of the way was when Brent stepped out into the open.

"You men just do as you're told and you'll live to finish your trip. Toss your guns over here. I know you're both packing side arms, so do it," Brent said in an even voice.

The men did as they were told and Brent then said, "Now call your passengers and tell them to pitch their guns over the side of the road and then walk over here."

"You won't get away with this, stranger. Besides we're not carrying anything worth stealing," Red said.

"Your passengers are; now do as I told you," Brent said, his voice taking on a little harder edge.

Red turned around and called out to the rest of his passengers, "You folks all get out of the coach. You men toss your guns over the side of the road, then walk over here. We're being held up."

The passengers consisted of two women and three men, counting Mr. Rubio. One of the women was Mrs. Rubio and the other woman was a dancehall girl who had been run out of the town where she had worked. The two remaining men were brothers on their way to a horse auction where they were hoping to buy a stud for breeding purposes.

The men all tossed their guns over the side of the road and made the short walk over to where the others were.

Brent eyed the dancehall woman questioningly; who gave him a hard stare in return.

"You wouldn't be packing a Derringer in that handbag would you, lady," Brent asked the dancehall woman?

"I would not. Do you want to look for yourself?"

"No, I'll take your word for it. The rest of you put your money in this gentleman's hat," Brent said reaching over and knocking Mr. Rubio's hat off his head.

Rubio bristled, but didn't say anything.

Everyone slowly began to take out their valuables, but Brent spoke up, "Ladies, you can keep whatever is in those handbags. It's just the men's money I want."

"You won't get away with this, mister," one of the brothers said.

"So far, so good," Brent said. "Now dig."

The two brothers looked at one another and tossed their wallets into the hat. Mr. Rubio, too, tossed his wallet into his hat. Brent continued to eye the two brothers who continued to cast a quick glance at one another. Brent stated, "I think you boys are holding out on me."

"We gave you our wallets; what more do you want," one of the men said asked?

"What you have under your coats. Unbutton 'em," Brent ordered.

The two men looked from Brent to one another as they slowly unbuttoned their coat buttons.

"Come on, pull the coat back so I can see which one of you is wearing the money belt," Brent said motioning with his pistol.

"You'll pay for this. We won't forget you, Bad man," one of the men said with clenched teeth as he pulled his coat open exposing the money belt he had around his middle.

"Drop it to the ground," Brent said in a calm voice. He then looked at Mr. Rubio who was also dressed in a business suit, "You too, hoss. Open up your coat."

Mr. Rubio slowly opened his coat and sticking out of his vest pocket was the grip of a Derringer. Brent grinned followed with a light chuckle.

"Take that pop gun out using your thumb and forefinger, and toss it over with the money. And then open your vest," Brent said dropping the grin.

Rubio opened his vest exposing his own money belt. Brent motioned with his gun and the man took it off and dropped it with the others valuables.

"I'll hire a bounty hunter to find you and I'll pay him a thousand dollars to bring you in dead," Mr. Rubio said angrily.

"I hope you don't try to hold out on him like you tried to on me," Brent replied.

"I'll see you dead if it's the last thing I ever do," Rubio went on.

Brent's expression changed to a hard stare, but as he had a thought it went back to one of almost amusement.

"You and I are about the same size. How about taking off that coat," Brent ordered.

A questioning look came to Rubio's face, but he slowly took off his suit coat.

"Go ahead; drop it on the ground...so you can take off the vest and shirt," Brent said with steely eyes.

"What, what do you want them for," Rubio asked?

"Just do as your told or I'll have your wife take her clothes off as well," Brent snapped angrily.

Rubio cast a quick glance at his wife and then removed his vest and shirt. When he was through he looked angrily at Brent.

Brent smiled as he said, "You guessed it, hoss; now the pants."

Rubio took a deep breath and gritted his teeth. Slowly he began to remove his pants. Brent kept a close eye on the others, only glancing towards Rubio occasionally to make sure he was obeying him.

"You shouldn't humiliate a man this way, hombre," Corky, the guard said. 'Taking their money is bad enough; you don't have to add insult to injury."

"Maybe you'd like to finish the trip in your long johns," Brent snapped.

Corky's eyes widened, "No," he said quickly.

"Then keep quiet. You've all been very cooperative up to this point, so don't anyone go spoiling it for the others. Just keep doing as you're told and we'll get along just fine. This gentleman threatened me, and I don't like to be threatened," Brent said and then motioned towards the stagecoach.

"Now you can all climb back aboard the coach and be on your way," he said with a smile.

"Are you going to send us on without any weapons? We've heard that a Comanche war party is in the area," Corky said with a frown.

"I'll tell you what I'll do because I'm such a nice guy. I'll give you your cartridges, but I'll take the guns and drop them at that big tree by the side of the road up ahead. You just make sure you don't move that coach until I wave back to you," Brent said thoughtfully. "Now go back and load up."

They all looked at him for a moment before turning and slowly walking back to the coach. Brent grinned at the sight of Mr. Rubio walking along in boots and long johns. He more than likely had more clothes in their baggage; if not he would be the talk of the town when they arrived at their destination.

While they were loading up, Brent picked up the wallets and money belts, and emptied their contents into his saddlebags that he had brought down the hill with him. He wadded up Rubio's clothes and stuck them under his arm.

Casting a quick glance at the passengers as they loaded up, he waited until everyone was aboard the coach before moving back up the hill to where his horse was tied. He put his saddlebags behind the saddle and then his bedroll. Rubio's clothes, he tied atop the bedroll. A business man's suit might come in handy, he thought.

Once he was loaded up he road down to where the passengers were waiting and went about unloading all the guns. He tossed the cartridges into the stagecoach's boot well and then ran a piece of rawhide he had removed from his saddlebags, through the trigger guards, stringing all the guns together. He looked back at the coach and its passengers and gave tip of his hat.

"Adios," he called out as he kicked his horse into an easy lope up the road in the direction of the big tree. When he reached it he dropped the guns by the side of the road and gave a wave back to the coach.

Raymond D. Mason

8

BUSTER RAWLINGS watched Brian Sackett from his upstairs bedroom window. His father's guest was replacing the horseshoe his horse had thrown. A deep set scowl covered Buster's face to such a degree that it appeared painful.

As Buster watched Sackett he was further upset when his sister, Barbie, walked out from the house to join Sackett.

"What's she doing," Buster muttered under his breath.

Barbie walked up to where Brian was and stopped just out of his view. Sensing someone was there, BJ looked back and when he saw it was Barbie, set the horse's hoof down on the ground.

"Well, good morning. I want to thank you again for that fine supper last night. You are really quite a good cook," BJ said with a smile.

"Oh, thank you. I learned to cook from my mother. She was a great cook."

"I just finished putting a shoe on my horse so I can leave right after the barbeque tomorrow," BJ said wondering if that was what she wanted to know.

"I guess you're anxious to get home, huh? It's a long ride to Abilene. I hope you don't run into any trouble," she said and then corrected herself, "Or should I say 'any more' trouble. I'm still sorry about the way my brother acted and I'm so thankful that you didn't let it go too far."

"It was more a question of you not letting it go too far. He wasn't letting up on me until you walked in," BJ said, wanting to give her the credit for Buster's cowardice.

Barbie smiled and lowered her eyes. She was just about to say something when Buster walked up behind her and snapped, "You stay away from my sister, Sackett. She'll marry a man with class."

BJ looked at him and grinned, "Then she won't be marrying a man like me...or you. And just for your information, we hadn't even mentioned when, or, where our wedding would take place."

Barbie found the humor in Brian's remark and added to it, "Oh, but Brian darling, I have the guest list all made out and I'd like you to look at it."

Buster fumed, "Whose side are you on, anyway, Sis? I'm your brother!"

"Don't remind me. I'm ashamed of that fact when you act like this. Brian and I were merely talking and you come up and make a complete fool of yourself. I think you owe our guest an apology," Barbie said, her eyes flashing hot with anger.

"I don't need or want an apology; I just want you to stay away from me Buster. It's obvious that you don't like me and I'm not all that fond of you, so let's just avoid each other and we'll avoid trouble," Brian said calmly.

Buster glared at Brian and started to say something when Royce Rawlings walked up. He saw the look on his son's face and gave Brian a quick glance.

"So what are you young people up to," Royce asked?

"Just having a little discussion about our upcoming wedding," Barbie said looking from her father to Buster and then back to her father.

"Oh, and who is it that is getting married?'

"Buster seems to think it is Brian and me, don't you, Buster," Barbie said.

Royce smiled widely, "Well, I for one would be very happy to welcome Brian into our family. Wouldn't that be something; the Rawlings and the Sackett's tying the knot?"

Buster looked from his father to his sister and then to Brian and back again to his father.

"I think you're all crazy," Buster said and stormed away from the corral.

Royce started to say something but didn't. He merely watched his son stomp off in the direction of the barn.

"I'm going to have to have a serious talk with that young man," Royce said quietly.

"Father, Brian and I were merely talking when Buster walked up and told Brian to stay away from me. Sometimes I think that man has a demon."

"You maybe right there, Barbie. He takes after his uncle Dave on your mother's side and I always said that about him. He could get mad over spilling s drop of water, I swear," Royce said. "We tangled more than one time just after your mother and I got married."

"If my being here is going to cause this kind of trouble I can move on right away," Brian said. "I'm rested and I've put that shoe on my horse, so he's ready to go."

"You'll do no such a thing. You're our guest and I want you to have a good time before you head on back to Abilene," Royce said shaking his head no.

"I'd like for you to stay," Barbie said invitingly.

"Well now, that makes it all different," Brian said with a wide grin. "Don't worry; I'll give Buster a wide berth."

The sound of hoof beats made the three of them turn and look towards the barn. Buster had saddled his horse and kicked it into a full gallop, whipping the animal with the long bridle reins for even more speed.

"I swear he goes through a horse a week. Where do you suppose he's going at this time of day," Royce asked aloud?

"My guess is that he's either going into town or to August's," Barbie answered.

Royce looked quickly in his daughter's direction, "What do you know about August's place?"

"I'm not a child, Father. I've known about August's since I was fifteen years old," Barbie replied and then added, "I know that you make a trip over there every once in awhile."

"I thought I was being discreet about it. I hope you'll forgive me for my weakness, honey," Royce asked sorrowfully.

"You're not that old a man, Father. I understand, believe me. Just be careful," Barbie said with a smile.

Brian felt uncomfortable listening to the Rawlings' airing their dirty laundry and took the opportunity to excuse himself.

"You know I still have to rasp down the horse's hoof where I put that new shoe. If you'll excuse me, I'll just do it now." BJ said.

"I'm going to go after Buster and see if I can't sooth his ruffled feathers and get him home. I don't want him getting drunk and into trouble," Royce said.

"Do you want me to ride into town with you, Father," Barbie inquired?

"No, no, I'll be all right. I won't be gone long. Have a good day, Brian. I'll see you when I get back. Tomorrow's going to be a big day. We may just go right on over into Sunday, I don't know," Royce said with a wide smile.

Three Days to Sundown

Brent Sackett rode into the town of Segovia just before sundown. He tied up in front of the only hotel in town and grabbed his saddlebags and rifle and went inside. There was a Mexican woman seated behind a small counter wearing a peasant blouse pulled down over her shoulders, exposing a lot of her ample breasts.

Brent grinned at the woman and nodded his approval. She grinned back at him and asked, "What would you like, Meester; a bed, a companion, or both?"

"Just a bed right now," Brent replied. "The last thing I need is someone snoring so loud they'd keep me awake. Stick around though. I don't sleep all the time."

She showed him to his room and gave oa seductive look before leaving him alone. Brent looked around the room and shook his head at its simplicity.

"I'll be glad when I hit a bigger city," he said as he dropped his gear at the foot of the bed.

He took the only chair in the room and jammed it under the door knob. He didn't trust the lock on the door; besides she hadn't even given him a key. He chuckled lightly as that thought crossed his mind.

He pulled his boots off and removed his gun belt, but he slipped his pistol under his pillow as he lay back on the bed. Letting out a sigh, he was asleep within thirty seconds. He dreamed fitfully, but at least he slept. When he awoke it was almost midnight.

Still being fully clothed except for his boots made getting ready to go down to the small cantina easy. He put his boots on and grabbed his hat and gun belt and put them on and then pulled the back of the chair out from under the doorknob.

Just as he stepped out into the hallway he saw two men turn the corner and start towards their room which was across from his. He lowered his head slightly as he passed by the men. One of the men glanced at him in passing, but did a double take.

87

Once Brent had passed them, the man elbowed his friend, "Did you see who that was; it was Brent Sackett. He used to be the deputy sheriff in Crystal City. I went through there about a year ago and he was there then. I read not long ago where he's wanted for killing the man he worked for and took off with some stolen money," the man said rapidly to his friend.

"Are you sure that's him?"

"Yeah, I'm sure. I've stood as close to him as you and I are right now. I saw him cut a man down when the man decided he didn't want to be arrested and went for his gun. Sackett beat him by a full second."

"Shouldn't we do something if he's wanted by the law?"

"I know what we'll do; let's turn him into the sheriff. If there's a reward we'll get it for getting him placed under arrest."

"What are we waiting for; let's go."

The two men rushed down the street to the sheriff's office. They woke the sheriff, who was asleep in his chair, and told him their story. He checked his wanted posters and when he saw Sackett's paperwork folded it up and stuck it in his pocket; Then he grabbed a sawed off shotgun that was propped against the wall next to his desk. With the two men in tow, the sheriff went out to find the desperado named Brent Sackett.

Brent was sitting at a table in the small bar where he could watch the door. He had invited one of the two women in the bar to join him. They were engaged in light conversation when the sheriff and the two men with him entered the room. Brent noticed them immediately and slowly pulled his pistol out, holding it under the table out of sight.

He watched them with a steely eyed gaze as they looked around the room. When one of the men spotted Brent he held his hand up to his mouth and said something to the sheriff, who nodded and looked Brent's way. The three of them, then moved slowly towards Brent's table.

Brent cocked the hammer of his Colt back, but didn't let on he was aware of their presence. The woman with Brent heard the sound of the hammer being jacked back and looked quickly at Brent and then towards the men. She slowly started to get up out of her chair.

The two men with the sheriff stopped, but the sheriff continued on towards Brent. When he cocked the hammers back on the double barrel shotgun, Brent whipped his Colt out from under the table and shot the sheriff; hitting him in the chest.

The sheriff pulled the triggers on the shotgun, blowing a huge hole in the floor. Before the sheriff hit the floor Brent turned his gun on the two men who had come in with the sheriff. Both men were hit by the spray of bullets Brent fired; only one of the men had gotten a shot off and it went wild.

Brent gave the room a quick scan as he stood up and saw no one else going for their guns. He walked over to the sheriff and looked down at the man. The sheriff lay there with his eyes wide open and blank. One of the two men who had came in with the sheriff was still alive, but in bad shape.

Brent looked over at the bartender who was frozen in fear and said, "If there's a doctor in this town, you'd better get him. This one's still breathing."

"We got no doctor here," the bartender said.

"Too bad for him," Brent said and walked out of the bar.

He walked back to his room, picked up his saddlebags, rifle, and bedroll and went back out to the hitching rail. He holstered his rifle, secured the saddlebags behind the saddle; and tied the bedroll on. After tightening the cinch he mounted up and rode slowly out of town and into the night.

"You're going to have ten thousand dollars on your head if you kill any more lawmen," Brent said as a grin came to his face.

The grin faded quickly, however, when another thought forced its way to the front of his mind. "Ma and Pa," he said softly. The thought brought a frown. He'd come along way since he'd been a happy kid living on the ranch. Had the War changed him this much? He didn't know for sure. Maybe he'd always been this way?

"Maybe something else will come along that will turn me back the other way," he said to no one but himself.

9

THE RAWLINGS' YEARLY SHINDIG had just gotten underway when a fight broke out between a couple of the Rawlings hands who had an issue between them that had to be resolved. What better way than a good old fashioned fistfight.

BJ looked on with mild amusement as the two men tried desperately to make solid contact with the other's jaw, as they rolled around on the ground. Their flailing away at one another would only result in a couple of sore backs.

Buster walked up just as the fight was coming to a close, with both men huffing and puffing so much they had to stop their wild swinging to catch their breaths. The two men finally looked at one another in a long stare down and then both broke into laughter. The fight was over with no harm done.

"If you're going to fight, you should learn how," Buster said as he walked up to the two men who were still sitting on the ground.

"Oh, I thought we knew how; look how dirty we are," the shorter of the two men said, drawing a chuckle from the other man.

"You both disgust me. You've already got the party off to a bad start. Go clean up, you're both a disgrace," Buster went on.

"Oh, come on Buster, you know that every year something like this happens. It's a time to clear the air of any hard feelings. Luke and I will be getting drunk together in a little while," the man answered.

"Don't talk back to me or I'll show you how to fight," Buster said angrily.

Brian looked around to see if he could spot Royce Rawlings anywhere, but didn't see him or Barbie. He could tell that Buster was looking for trouble from anyone he felt he held an edge over. He couldn't help but shake his head negatively at the bullying tactics of Buster. His disgusted look didn't go unnoticed by young Rawlings.

"What're you looking at, Sackett," Buster snapped?

"Not much, from what I see," Brian said without hesitation.

"What do you mean by that crack," Buster said with a deep frown?

"Figure it out, Buster."

"I've watched you, Sackett. I don't think you're all that tough. You may have size, but you don't have the savvy that I do when it comes to fighting. Why don't you step out here and we'll show these cowhands how real men fight," Buster said confidently.

"Buster, you've never seen me fight, and you don't want too. All this is over that gal named Flo and we were just sitting and talking. I don't want to fight you, or anyone else on this ranch. My suggestion is that since I'll be leaving here tomorrow let's just let things between us cool off," Brian said.

"I say you're a coward," Buster said, looking around at the onlookers.

Brian's eyebrows knitted into a frown, "And I say you're a fool. You're wanting to showoff in front of your friends and all that's going to happen is you're going to get painfully embarrassed. Now drop it."

Buster grinned, "You must have fought on the side of the South in the War and you're afraid of losing again."

"And you must have not fought for either side; either that or you took a slug to the head and your brains have all leaked out," Brian came back.

"Nobody talks to me like that," Buster said and made a head long lunge for Brian.

Brian stepped to one side and put his hand on the back of Buster's head, and sent him sprawling to the ground. Before Buster could get up Brian moved around to where he was standing by one of the large tables near the barbeque pit.

Buster scrambled to his feet and whirled around. When he saw where Brian was standing he rushed him again. This time Brian grabbed a large skillet that was to be used for frying potatoes and hit Buster atop the head, knocking him out cold.

The onlookers broke out in applause when they saw that Buster was unconscious. The truth was none of the wranglers liked the rancher's son, but avoided a confrontation due to the good pay and working conditions Royce Rawlings offered.

Judd Hoover walked up to Brian and put his hand on his shoulder, "I want to give you a big 'thank you' from all the guys on the ranch who have wanted to do just that very thing. We didn't do it because of our love for Royce and the working conditions he provides. As for that little snot on the ground...if anything ever happens to his pa he won't have a ranch hand in Texas that would work for him."

"I'm not looking for trouble; I've had enough to last me a lifetime, but he just won't let up, will he?"

"Nope; we have to literally ride away from him when he gets like this. You tried to avoid any conflict; we all heard you," Judd said as he picked up a water bucket that was about half full.

Without another word, Judd moved over to Buster's prone body and poured the water on his face. Buster shook his head and blinked his eyes open. Once his vision cleared enough to focus on any one thing he got to his feet, holding his aching head.

Buster looked around and then stopped when he saw Brian. BJ grinned slightly and said, "I told you that you wouldn't like the way I fight."

Buster didn't say a word as he grabbed his hat off the ground and walked slowly away from the crowd. On his way to the ranch house he passed by Barbie who was bringing s few things from the kitchen. She paused as the two met, but nothing was said.

Walking up to Judd and Brian, Barbie asked, "Buster sure is in a somber mood today. How did his shirt get so wet?"

"Oh, he had a slight accident with a frying pan, and I splashed water in his face," Judd said casting a quick wink at Brian.

"Oh," Barbie said and moved on over to the barbeque pit. All those who had seen the scuffle chuckled lightly at Judd's explanation and Barbie's response.

Buster walked into the ranch house and closed his eyes from the pain caused by the headache he'd just been given. Royce Rawlings was coming out of the living room as Buster entered and saw the condition of his son.

"What happened, Buster; why are you so wet," Royce asked?

Buster's eyes flashed hot with anger as he replied through gritted teeth, "It's that Sackett friend of yours; he hit me with something and knocked me out. They poured water on me to wake me up. I'm going to go back and kill him; I came to get my guns."

"You leave those guns right where they are. There'll not be any killing on this ranch unless I order it done. Go upstairs and put a fresh shirt on and go back out to the get-together. I'll ask those that witnessed the incident what happened and if Brian Sackett was responsible for the trouble I'll have him leave the ranch immediately; if not, I'll have a talk with you," Royce said firmly.

"You never take my side on anything, do you, old man," Buster snapped.

"You haven't been on the right side of an issue in your entire life, Buster. You've always been a troublemaker just like you uncle. Now do as I say and get a fresh shirt on and then get your butt out to that shindig."

Buster glared at Royce for a moment and then whirled around and took the stairs two at a time up to his room. Royce shook his head as he grabbed his hat off the hat rack by the door and headed down to the gathering to find out what had happened.

"What happened out here, Judd," Royce asked when he walked up to the crowd?

"Nothing much, Boss. Buster went after Sackett here and Brian put him to sleep for a few seconds. I brought him around with a bucket of water. It really wasn't much," Judd replied.

"Buster started the incident?"

"Yep, Sackett tried to avoid it, but Buster wouldn't let up and finally rushed Brian. He was merely protecting himself and made short work of it," Judd said seriously.

Looking at Brian, Royce shook his head, "Brian I'm apologizing for my son's behavior again. I hope you'll accept it."

"I do, so let's just forget it ever happened. I'll be gone in the morning and that will allow things to settle down," BJ said with a slight grin.

"Let's have us a winging, what do you say," Royce said with a big smile?

"I'm all for that," BJ replied and gave a laugh.

"Barbie, how's that meat coming along; I'm so...," Royce said, but his words were cut off in mid sentence when Buster pushed his way through some of the guests carrying a double barreled shotgun.

With a crazed look on his face he growled, "I'm going to kill you, Sackett. Nobody humiliates me and gets away with it."

Royce spun around and glared at his son, "Put that gun down, Buster."

"Shut up, old man; I'm going to kill this no good son of a ...," Buster started to say just as one of the ranch hands grabbed the barrel of the gun and tried to wrest it away from Buster.

Suddenly there was a loud explosion of gunpowder as both barrels of the gun went off. The ranch hand had managed to get the gun out of Buster's hand all right, but in the process Royce was hit in the face with the buckshot. He fell to the ground, dead.

Barbie screamed as she ran to her father, but the gruesome sight caused her to stop and turn her face away. Three men grabbed Buster and held him, to keep him from running away. Brian and Judd quickly covered the body with a loose tarp lying nearby.

Judd took Royce's hand and felt for a pulse, knowing full well he would not find one. After several torturous seconds he looked at the onlookers and shook his head negatively.

"He's gone," Judd said.

"It's all his fault," Buster yelled out. "If he'd never come here, none of this would have happened. You all saw him knock me out awhile ago...it's his fault, not mine," Buster pleaded, but no one was listening to his plea.

"We'd better get the sheriff out here," Judd said and then added, "Slim, will you ride into town and tell Spud to get out here right away?'

"I'm on my way, Judd," Slim said and ran towards the corral.

Brian looked at Barbie who was sitting on the ground and crying her eyes out. He moved over and knelt down beside her, putting his arm around her shoulder. Several of the women who were present had also moved over to console the sobbing Barbie.

"I'm so sorry for all this," Brian said softly. "Your father was a good man."

"He's gone, he's gone," Barbie cried. "Why, how...oh, my God," she cried.

"Now, now honey, you just go ahead and let it all out," one of the women said.

Brian gave way for the women, feeling they would know better how to console her than a man would. He looked at Buster and felt his blood run cold. He walked across to where the men were restraining Buster and scowled as he looked into Buster's eyes.

"You've wanted to kill someone for so long, punk; how does it feel. You're a real killer now, you squirrel eyed little snot. I should beat you to death, but I won't. No, I'll leave that for someone else to do. And it will happen. You'll mouth off to the wrong man one of these days and he'll send you to hell. I hope you live a long time, though. I want you to dream about this day forever. I want you to see your father's faceless body in your mind's eye every time you see a shotgun or hear a gunshot," Brian spewed.

Turning to Judd, Brian said, "Judd, I'll be leaving today. I can't stay around here. I'm sorry for all of this, but, Junior here, wouldn't leave me alone."

"We all know that, Brian. Have a good ride home," Judd said evenly.

"Tell Barbie how sorry I am and if she ever gets up Abilene way, please stop in to see us," Brian said as he cast a quick look in her direction.

Just then there was a commotion with the men who had been restraining Buster. When BJ turned and looked in their direction he saw that Buster had broken free from the men's grip and was running towards several saddled horses. Before anyone could stop him, he swung into the saddle and rode away from the ranch in a cloud of dust.

"Let him go," Judd called out. "There's been enough upheaval today."

"Judd, take care," Brian said as he offered Hoover his hand, and as they shook hands he added, "Once Barbie is over the shock of all this I hope you'll tell her how sorry I am about everything."

"I will, Brian. As I said before, "Take care."

Brian walked up to the bunkhouse and grabbed his bedroll and rifle and then went to the barn and saddled his horse. He hated to leave Barbie like this, but knew he wouldn't be able to help her as much as the women here would. Besides he felt somewhat guilty about being part of the reason for Royce's death.

As he rode away from the ranch house he gave one last look back at the crowd of revelers turned mourners and hung his head. "Comfort her, Lord, comfort her," he said softly.

Brent Sackett crested a hill and looked down on the three covered wagons that were stopped in a small grove of trees. It struck him as odd that the wagons were not on the main road, but a good mile away from it.

He figured them to be homesteaders. He also figured they might be good for a hot meal as he kicked his horse up and rode down the hill to where they were camped.

As Brent rode along his observations told him something wasn't right. He observed that the horses were not hobbled, and were grazing on high grass, a good, hundred and fifty yards away from the wagons. He didn't see anyone around the campsite either.

When he reached the first wagon he called out, "Hello; is anybody here," but got no answer? Again he called out, "Hey, is anyone around here?" Still, there was no answer.

Brent climbed out of the saddle and looked towards the campfire. That's when he noticed the way the skillet was upside down on the ground and the coffee pot was lying on its side. Something was definitely not right here. He pulled his pistol, thinking that this might possibly be the work of a Comanche war party. He doubted it, however, because they usually burned the wagons.

Cautiously, Brent moved up to the lead wagon and slowly opened up the rear canvas flap. There was a man lying face down in a small puddle of blood. From the looks of it he had been shot several times and the exit wounds had blown a huge hole in his back.

Quickly Brent walked to the next wagon in line and climbed up on the bench seat. Lying off to the left side of the wagon he saw another man's body. He, too, had been shot several times. Looking inside the wagon, Brent saw the body of a woman; probably the man's wife; she was dead. It appeared to him that she had been raped and then shot one time in the chest.

Brent covered the woman's body with a blanket in the wagon and then went to the last wagon. Before he reached it, however, he heard a slight moan. It came from inside the wagon, so he scrambled up onto the bench seat. He looked inside the wagon and saw a young blonde woman badly beaten and wounded. She had been shot in the shoulder, but she was alive.

Knowing there was nothing he could do for the others Brent began working on the wounded woman. Whoever had done this must have thought the gunshot had killed her. He could see right away that the bullet would have to be removed. As he climbed out the back he found another man lying about ten yards behind the wagon. Like the others, he too, had been shot several times with a high powered rifle; maybe a buffalo gun.

He made the woman as comfortable as possible and then climbed out of the wagon to build a fire so he could begin removing the bullet in her shoulder. He noticed right away that the horse's hoof prints around the wagons were not Indian ponies, but were all shod. Indian's do not put horseshoes on their horses. This was done by white men.

Brent built a fire and found a pot. When he went to get water out of the water barrels on the wagons he found that all of them had bullet holes in them. He was able to find enough water at the very bottom of the barrels, however, to fill several buckets of water.

Brent went to the wagon and found that woman had stopped moaning and was in a deeper unconscious state than before. He also noticed something else about the woman; she was beautiful. She was also wearing a wedding ring.

Fortunately the unconscious woman had been shot by a handgun and not with a rifle like the others had been. He was able to get the bullet out with no trouble, but the wound began to bleed very badly. He'd have to cauterize the wound in order to stop the bleeding.

He found a metal stoker and after cleaning it, began to heat it. It would work good as a tool to use in searing the wound shut. He hated to do it, but didn't know of anything else he could do. Having to perform this on such a beautiful woman made him feel sick to his stomach. But, he did it and he did a good job under the circumstances.

Brent carried the woman back to the wagon and lay her down very gently. He covered her up and made her as comfortable as possible. It was only then that he set about burying the others.

By the time he'd finished burying the dead his patient was beginning to come around enough that he could ask her a few questions. Brent was leaning over her when she awoke. Her first impulse was to strike out blindly and wildly at who she believed to be her attackers.

"Hold on, Ma'am, I'm here to help you," Brent said as she flailed away at him and he fended her off.

"You killers, I hate you," the woman said as Brent held both of her wrists..

"Calm down, lady; I am going to help you," he said.

The pain in her shoulder caused her to stop striking out at the man who had probably saved her life. Had Brent not come along, the woman would have bled to death.

"Can you tell me what happened here, Ma'am," Brent asked in a soothing voice.

The woman didn't say anything at first, but after a few long seconds finally said, "They killed them. They killed them."

Her eyes held a vacant stare due to what she had been forced to witness. "They whipped me; whipped me something awful."

"Who did this to you, Ma'am," Brent asked?

The woman turned and looked through Brent, then slowly shook her head yes.

"Riders for Kennard," she said evenly, her expression not changing.

"You mean to tell me that cowhands did this," Brent questioned?

She slowly shook her head yes and then burst into tears, burying her face in her hands. Brent felt very bad for the woman and put his hand on her shoulder.

"I'll stay with you and make sure you get to where ever it is you want to go," Brent said hoping to relieve some of the fear and uncertainty she was feeling right then.

"Ma'am, I'm going to get out now, and fix us something to eat. Are you hungry," he asked?

The woman managed to say no, that all she wanted to do was go to sleep. Brent told her that he would be right outside the wagon if she needed anything, to which she was actually able to force a faint smile of thanks.

Brent found some potatoes and salt pork in one of the wagons, along with a can of lard. He also found some other items he could use. It wasn't a gourmet meal, but it was good enough tasting and would stick to a person's ribs.

Before bedding down for the night, Brent checked on the woman and found her sound asleep. He unsaddled his horse and made sure it was secure before turning in. His head no sooner hit the pillow he took from one of the wagons, than he was sound asleep, as well.

During the night, Brent heard the woman sobbing loudly. He quickly got up and looked inside the wagon. She was moving her head from side to side as she fought off someone in her dreams.

Afraid she would reopen the wound he had cauterized; Brent climbed into the wagon and tried to restrain the woman. Suddenly she opened her eyes and the look on her face was one of terror. She screamed thinking Brent was one of the men who had killed the others and thought they had killed her.

"It's all right, Ma'am, it's all right. No one is going to hurt you. I am here to help you; I'm your friend," Brent said in his attempt to calm the woman's fears.

"Please don't...please don't hurt me anymore," she said and began to weep.

"No one is going to hurt you, Ma'am. I'll see to that. My name is Brent Sackett...," Brent said before catching himself.

He hadn't meant to say his real name, but in her condition she probably wouldn't remember it anyway. The struggle caused the wound to weep slightly, but it didn't reopen much. Brent felt the woman relax suddenly as she once again slipped into unconsciousness. This time she was out until sunrise.

Brent had a pot of coffee on when the woman slowly peered around the back corner of the wagon. She watched Brent quietly for over a minute. She looked all around the area to make sure he was alone before letting him know that she was awake.

The smell of coffee brewing and bacon frying made her realize how hungry she was. Only then did she truly realize that she had been bandage up. Now she knew for sure that this man wasn't one of those who had attacked them.

"Hello," she said cautiously.

Brent looked quickly towards the sound of the woman's weak voice and smiled, "Hello. How do you feel this morning," he asked, not really knowing what else to say?

"I hurt all over. Who are you, mister," she asked?

Brent felt relief that she had not remembered what he had told her the night before, "Dan..., uh, Dan Burton," he said figuring that the name Dan Johnson would no longer be a name he could go by. "What happened here, Ma'am, if you don't mind talking about it?"

"Are the others...," she started to say, but couldn't bring herself to ask if they were all dead.

Brent lowered his head and nodded slowly, "I'm afraid so, Ma'am. I buried them yesterday."

"John...Peggy...George; Luke...all dead; the men wouldn't stop...they wouldn't stop," she said closing her eyes at the thought.

She turned her face heavenward as tears burst out of her eyes and streamed down her face. She moaned slightly from the pain of grief she felt in her heart. She bit her lower lip and tried to keep herself from going all to pieces. Brent saw her pain and hoped to get her mind off the subject for the time being.

"I think this bacon is done. I found a few eggs in one of the wagons. How do you like them," he asked?

Pulling herself together she managed to say, "Over easy," and started to climb out of the wagon.

Brent saw what she was attempting to do and rushed to the back of the wagon, saying "Hold on, Ma'am. Let me help you out of there."

Brent put his hands around her small waist and lifted her down out of the wagon. She looked into his eyes as he gently set her down.

"Thank you so much for your kindness, Mr. Burton. You saved my life," she said.

"Well, I don't know about that; it was nothing more than anyone in my position would have done," Brent said sounding almost too humble to his way of thinking.

Quickly he added, "Who did this, anyway?"

The woman's eyes narrowed slightly, "Riders from the Crooked K; violent men."

Brent felt a stirring in his heart as he watched and listened to the woman. He still didn't even know her name, but he felt a kind of kinship to her. He'd never had this kind of feeling towards a woman before. This was something different; something good. He wasn't sure, but he felt like he loved her at first sight. To him, she was the most beautiful woman on the face of the Earth.

10

BJ SACKETT reined his horse up in front of the Yellow Rose Saloon. It was getting late in the day and all he wanted was to have a cold beer and a bite to eat. His mind was still filled with thoughts of Royce Rawlings and what had happened back at the Double R.

Pushing through the batwing doors, BJ sidled up to the bar and waited for the bartender to make his way down to him. Being late in the day, the small saloon was about half full. There were a couple of card game going on and a banjo player picking out 'Camp Town Racetrack'.

"What'll it be, stranger," the barkeep asked, giving Brian a quizzical look?

"Beer," Brian said working his neck from side to side to get the kinks out.

"Where you from," the bartender asked as he drew the beer?

"Up near Abilene," BJ replied.

"Did you come out of San Antone," the man continued to question?

"Yeah, yeah I did, as a matter of fact," BJ said, wondering why all the questions.

"You must have come up through Medina then, is that right?"

Brian eyed the man suspiciously, "Yeah, I did. Are you writing a book on my travels," BJ asked with a slight grin?

"Nope, just making small talk," the bartender said as he set the glass of beer in front of BJ. "That'll be a nickel."

BJ put a dime out on the counter, "I'll be having another beer when this one is gone."

The bartender took the dime and walked down to the cash register and rang up the sale of two beers. BJ noticed him say something to one of the women that worked in the saloon and she gave BJ a quick glance and nodded.

"I'm about to have company," Brian said under his breath.

Instead of coming down the bar to where he was standing, the woman went out the front door. "Guess I was wrong," BJ said with a grin.

He had just finished his first glass of beer and started on his second when the woman re-entered the saloon. She wasn't alone, however. Alongside her was the sheriff of Kerrville. He walked up behind BJ with his gun drawn and spoke.

"Turn around real slow and don't even think about going for that gun," the sheriff said.

Brian slowly looked around to make sure he was the one being addressed. When he saw the sheriff standing there, he did as he had been told to do.

"What's this all about," Brian asked?

"Is your name Brian Sackett," the lawman asked?

"Yes, I'm Brian Sackett. Why," he replied?

"You're under arrest, mister; for the murder of Royce Rawlings," the sheriff said flatly.

"For the murder...I didn't kill Royce Rawlings, his son, Buster, killed him," Brian snapped.

"That's not the story we got, and what we were told is that is exactly what you would say," the sheriff said as he motioned for the bartender to move back to where Sackett was standing.

"Now I want you to put your gun on the bar and step away from it," the sheriff ordered.

"Sheriff, you're making a big mistake. There were two dozen people saw what happened at the Rawlings ranch. They'll all testify that Buster is the one who shot his father," Brian said firmly, with a deep frown.

"Just do as I tell you and don't give me any lip," the sheriff said cocking the hammer back on his pistol.

Brian slowly removed his pistol and laid it on the bar, where the bartender picked it up and then stepped away.

"I'm taking you to jail, Sackett. Come on," the sheriff ordered with a wave of his pistol.

"Would you believe Barbie Rawlings and Judd Hoover, the Rawlings' foreman," Brian asked?

"Look, right now all I want to do is get you behind bars. I'll worry about statements from others after that. Now let's go."

Brian walked ahead of the sheriff and upon passing the young woman who had brought the sheriff back with her, he grinned as he said, "Thanks, honey."

The woman looked away quickly. When Brian reached the sidewalk he saw who was responsible for his arrest. Sitting on the horse he had taken from the ranch when he broke free, was Buster Rawlings. He stared at Brian who stared back.

"That's him, Sheriff; that's the man who murdered my father. I say we string him up right now. I'm your eyewitness to the murder," Buster said rapidly.

"Buster, you scum sucking pig; you killed your father and stole that horse your sittin' on," Brian growled with a deep set frown.

"I'll lock him up, Buster. Spud is on his way up here from Medina. I guess he'll take him back and hold him in jail there," the sheriff said.

"Keep a close eye on him, Sheriff; he's a dangerous man," Buster said with a twisted grin on his narrow face.

Brian started to say something but thought better of it. He had quickly deduced what was going on here. He knew that Spud Winters and Buster were very close and that Buster had more than likely gone to him and together they had come up with a plan. If Winters came here to Kerrville to take him back to Medina, it would be very easy to shoot him down in cold blood along the way somewhere, and claim he had tried to escape.

Brian knew he would have to make an escape before Winters showed up. It might be hard to do, what with Buster staying here to make sure he didn't get away. How Buster planned on dealing with all the other witnesses to the shooting was immaterial at the moment. He would probably try to use fear and intimidation to get them to change their eyewitness accounts of what happened. It would be very easy to do with the local law on his side.

The sheriff locked Brian in the lone cell the small jail had and went to his desk and sat down. Buster had told the sheriff he would be back after awhile and had headed for the Yellow Rose Saloon. He had something up his sleeve and it wasn't merely his arm.

"I say there's no need for a trial where some shifty lawyer can get this killer off Scot free," Buster said to the bar patrons that he had just bought a round of drinks for.

"Yeah, yeah," the crowd agreed.

"I say we string the murderer up right here in Kerrville and send a message to any other drifters that they can't kill one of our own and get away with it," Buster said loudly.

The bartender was one of few who didn't like the idea of a lynching. He had witnessed one in Wichita, Kansas and wanted nothing to do with another one. The only other one to be opposed to what Buster was stirring up was the woman who had gone for the sheriff. Her name was Kitty and she too had seen a lynching before.

"That man in the jail over there shot my father in the face with a shotgun and is now trying to say I did it. I wasn't even at the ranch," Buster lied. "He told everyone who was present at the party that if they identified him as the shooter he would come back and kill them all, one by one."

"I agree with Buster, let's string him up," someone yelled out from the crowd.

"Hang him and hang him high," another man chimed in.

"I say you men wait until the circuit judge comes next week. Let the judge hear both sides of what happened," the bartender called out.

"Yeah, and then let Sackett's lawyer get him off with no more than a slap on the hand. No, we've all seen too many miscarriages of justice around here. We ain't taking no chances of that happening here," Buster yelled out inciting the crowd; and then added. "Set up another round of drinks for my friends, here."

The bartender knew that a drunken crowd soon becomes an uncontrollable mob. He could see exactly what Buster was doing and felt he had to do something to stop it.

He motioned for Kitty to come over to the end of the bar. Whispering so none of the boisterous crowd could hear him, he said, "Go and tell the sheriff what's happening over here. These guys are going to get liquored up and storm the jail before long."

"Okay, but what if the sheriff doesn't come?"

"We'll worry about that if and when it happens. He should be made aware of what's taking place here though."

"Joe, I don't ever want to see another lynching. The one I saw wound up with the entire town being destroyed. Drunks were setting fire to stores and homes. It was terrible," Kitty said.

"I know; there's never any real good comes out of it. It would be better if this Sackett gets away than for him to be strung up without a trial. Wait a minute," the bartender said and gave a quick glance at the mob that was being fired up.

He went to the cash register and opened it up, and after another quick glance over his shoulder, took the Derringer out and slipped it into his vest pocket. He closed the register and moved back over to Kitty.

"If the sheriff doesn't seem too interested in stopping this craziness, slip this to Sackett somehow," he said as he passed the Derringer to her unseen.

"Do you think this is a good idea," Kitty asked?

"Do you want to see another lynching?"

She shook her head no and moved towards the batwings.

Noticing her departure, Buster called out, "Where are you going, Kitty? The fun's just beginning."

"I have to run an errand, Buster. I'll be back before the fun really gets underway," she replied.

"We're going to stretch a man's neck this far," Buster said as he held his hands a foot apart.

Kitty hurried down the street giving thought to what she was about to do. Did she really want to be involved in helping this stranger escape from jail? If they found out she had anything to do with it, both Joe and she could be held as accomplices. Before reaching the jail she knew what she would do.

Looking around to make sure that no one was watching, Kitty moved around to the back of the jail. She had spent a night in jail once, herself, and knew that there was a small window high up in the lone cell. If she could get the Derringer through it, it would fall straight down to the cot and no one would know how Sackett came by it.

Working quietly she found some empty crates by the building next to the jail and moved them under the small window. Carefully she climbed up on the crates until she could reach the open barred window.

She looked around to make sure the coast was still clear before dropping the Derringer through the bars of the window. The small gun landed on BJ's chest causing him to bolt upright, sending the Derringer clattering to the floor.

"What's going on back there," the sheriff called out from his desk?

Noticing it was a Derringer, BJ quickly replied, "Nothing, Sheriff; I just dropped the tin plate that was in here."

"Dam it, I told that so called deputy of mine not to leave that metal plate in the cell," the sheriff growled.

BJ quickly grabbed up the Derringer and broke it down to see if it was loaded. It wasn't. He snapped the barrel back in place and figured he could bluff his way out of jail. At least it was worth a try.

As he thought out his plan of escape he couldn't help but wonder if this was a set up by Buster. If he was able to bust out of jail by using the Derringer, Buster and others could be waiting for him outside and the moment he showed himself, gun him down.

He knew he would be taking a chance, but if Spud Winters got here from Medina his chances of survival would be even less than they were now. He would go ahead and try to make his break here.

"Sheriff, could I have some water," BJ asked?

"What do you need water for," the sheriff asked?

"I'm dehydrated. I guess I shouldn't have had those two beers. I sure would appreciate a cup of water," Brian asked politely.

"All right, all right; wait a minute," the sheriff groused.

The sheriff got a dipper full of water and moved to the jail cell. He held the dipper out as though he was going to give it to Brian through the open area in the bars that they used to pass the prisoners their plate of food through.

When BJ went to reach for the dipper, the sheriff threw the water in his face.

"Here's your water, killer," he said with a smirk on his face.

Brian bristled, "And here's yours, Sheriff," he said as he raised the empty Derringer and pointed it at the lawman.

The sheriff's eyes widened as the realization that his prisoner had the drop on him hit him.

"Where'd you get that," he asked, fear registering in his voice?

"Never mind that, give me your gun or I'll give you a couple of bullets through your head," Brian snapped.

"Yes, sir, Mr. Sackett, yes sir. Here," the sheriff said and quickly handed his gun to Brian through the open slot. "Just be careful with that thing; don't shoot."

Brian took the sheriff's gun and quickly checked to see if it was loaded. It was and that eased his mind about this whole thing being a set up.

"Now open this jail cell and be quick about it. You'd hate to get killed with your own gun wouldn't you, Sheriff?"

"I'd hate to get killed by anyone's gun," the sheriff said and quickly pulled the key from his pocket and opened the jail cell.

"Now get in here," Brian said as he grabbed his hat and moved outside the jail cell.

With the sheriff now behind bars, Brian locked the cell door and scowled at the sheriff.

"I didn't kill Mr. Rawlings, Sheriff. Buster killed his father accidentally and is trying to lay the shooting off on me. Now I want you to remain quiet until I've gone; do you hear me?"

"I hear you, Mr. Sackett. I'll be as quiet as a church mouse," the sheriff said honestly and then added, "I never wanted to be sheriff, but they elected me. I ain't no hero."

"Here, you might want to keep this as a souvenir," Brian said and tossed the Derringer into the jail cell.

"What the...," the sheriff said as he watched the gun slide across the floor.

"Adios, Sheriff," BJ said, and headed towards the sheriff's desk, where his gun and holster had been put into the bottom drawer when they came in.

BJ quickly buckled his gun belt on and checked his own gun to see if it was loaded; it was. Now if he could just get out of town without being seen, he thought. He opened the door just enough to peek outside and see if he could spot an ambush.

He saw no sign of life except for the noise drifting down the street from the Yellow Rose Saloon. BJ felt confident that this was not a set up for an ambush and cautiously moved out of the sheriff's office onto the boardwalk in front.

Looking down the street he saw that his horse was still tied at the hitching rail in front of the Yellow Rose Saloon. He didn't want to be charged with horse stealing unless it was absolutely necessary, so he crossed the street and moved up against the building across from the sheriff's office.

Staying in the shadows he moved along in the direction of the saloon. He was about twenty yards from his horse when the lynch mob came out onto the boardwalk; yelling and hollering for someone to 'get a rope'.

Buster had finally worked the men into a drunken frenzy and they were ready to throw a 'necktie party'. Brian quickly darted between two buildings before anyone in the mob spotted him. One of the men in the crowd, who's horse was tied next to Brian's, grabbed a rope off his saddle and held it high.

"I've got the rope with that killer's name on it," the man called out loudly.

"Come on, let's get him," Buster yelled, continuing to fan the flames of hate he'd created.

BJ waited until the men had moved in the direction of the jail before hurrying over to the hitching rail where his horse was tied. He swung into the saddle and started to rein his horse around when he looked at the saloon doorway. His heart skipped a beat when he saw the man and woman standing there and looking straight at him.

For a moment the three of them just stared at each other. And then, both the man and the woman smiled. It was the bartender and Kitty. Brian sensed they had something to do with the Derringer being dropped into his jail cell. He gave them a friendly tip of the hat and rode off into the night.

11

BRENT SACKETT drove the woman's wagon into the small town of Eden. His horse was tied to the back of the wagon. He had learned that the woman's name was Julia Summers. Her husband, John, and his brother George had bought a small ranch near Lubbock and were moving there when they were attacked by wranglers who worked for one of the biggest ranchers in the area, Ben Kennard. Peggy Summers was George's wife and Luke Clemens was a friend of theirs who was making the move with them.

Kennard had told them they could cross his land, but to keep moving. If he caught them on his range after 48 hours, he would burn their wagons. They would have been across his land, but one of the wagons broke a wheel and they had to stop and try to fix it. They thought Kennard would understand their situation and allow them more time. Obviously he wasn't an understanding man.

Brent didn't press her too much for details, knowing that she was still suffering from shock. He was able to piece the story together over the entire trip into Eden. From time to time she'd sob lightly as she recalled her ordeal.

The more Julia talked, the deeper the dislike Brent felt for this Ben Kennard. He found himself wishing he would run into the man while in Eden. Brent was falling in love with Julia and having a difficult time dealing with these new found emotions. One thing was clear to him; he didn't want her out of his life.

Luckily Eden had a doctor, or at least someone who practiced medicine. The local blacksmith gave them directions to the doctor's office, which was a small building in back of his house. Brent found it with no trouble and stopped near a small hitching rail.

Julia's lash marks made it difficult for her to move about, and the gunshot wound added to her inability to move freely. Brent climbed down off the wagon and told Mrs. Summers that he would check and see if the doctor was in.

"I'll just be a minute, Mrs. Summers. You just rest there until I see the doctor," Brent said with a kind smile.

"I can come in with you," Julia said.

"No, you don't strain yourself. I'll be right back. It looks like he's in; there's two horses tied at the hitching rail," Brent said as he looked towards the horses.

Suddenly his blood ran cold. One of the horses tied at the rail had the crooked *K* brand on it. Brent checked the other horse, but found no brand on it. One of the men was riding a horse from Kennard's ramuda. Brent went back to the wagon and asked Julia a question.

"Mrs. Summers, was one of the men who attacked you riding a big pinto?"

Julia closed her eyes as tears formed, "Yes, the man who shot John was. He laughed crazily," she said and began to weep.

Brent's jaws tightened as he walked back towards the building that held the sign 'Doctor's Office'. When he reached the front door he stopped and pulled his pistol out and checked to make sure it had a full load. Seeing that it did, he twirled the gun on his finger and let it fall back into his holster.

The two men looked towards the door as Brent opened it and entered. One of the men was seated and the other was being attended to by the doctor. Brent looked at both men with a scowl on his face. They returned the glare.

"I'll be right with you, young man," the doctor said as he carefully placed the bandage over the severe scratch marks on the man's face. "I'm just finishing up here."

Brent gave the seated man another glance and then looked back at the man standing by the doctor, "I have a lady outside that needs your attention, Doc. She's in bad shape," Brent said watching the reaction of the two cowboys.

"Oh, what seems to be her problem," the doctor asked?

"She was attacked by some low down rattlesnakes," Brent said and paused. "In fact four people traveling with the woman were all attacked by a bunch of scum sucking pigs. She's the only one who survived," Brent said as he felt his pulse rate quicken.

The two cowboys cast a quick glance at one another and then the one seated slowly got to his feet. Brent saw in the man's eyes that he knew exactly what he was talking about; and that they were in fact, part of the bunch to which he was referring.

"Rattlesnakes; scum sucking pigs," the doctor said curiously?

The man who had been seated was the first one to go for his gun. He never got it completely out of his holster before Brent shot and killed him. The man being attended to grabbed the doctor and pulled him around in front of him as a shield as he went for his gun. It was no use. Brent whirled and fired one shot that hit the cowboy in the forehead.

The back of the man's head exploded as the .44 slug exited. The doctor's eyes were as big as saucers as he looked quickly around his small office. He stuttered and stammered until Brent snapped angrily, 'There's nothing you can do for this vermin now, Doc. Take a look at the woman they shot."

It took the doctor several minutes to collect his wits. Brent didn't wait for him to do it, however, he grabbed the doctor by the arm and ushered him out of the office towards the wagon where Julia was waiting.

"She needs looking after," Brent said as he pulled the doctor along.

The doctor's wife opened the front door as they passed by the house and called out to her husband, "What was all the shooting about," she asked?

Brent called back to her, "It was nothing, Ma'am. I just had to kill a couple of rattlesnakes."

"Rattlesnakes, oh my Gosh; I hate those things," the woman said and quickly slammed the door shut.

The doctor climbed into the back of the wagon and started attending to Julia's wounds.

"Let me take a look at you, young lady. I hear you've had an accident," the doctor said kindly.

"It wasn't an accident, Doctor; it was intentional," Brent said as the doctor began to unbutton Julia's blouse so he could check the wound.

Brent moved away from the back of the wagon, but remained where he could hear and talk to the doctor.

As he worked on her the doctor asked, "You mean to tell me that those two men did this to her?"

Them and several others," Brent replied. "If I hadn't come along when I did, I don't think she would have made it."

"I'd say you're right. Did you cauterize the wound," the doctor asked?

"Yes, I did. Did I do a bad job?"

"A bad job; no, not at all," the doctor remarked, "On the contrary, you did a good job."

"The wranglers from the Crooked K killed this woman's husband, his brother and his wife, and a family friend. I'd like to press charges with the local sheriff or marshal here in Eden," Brent said firmly.

"No, I don't think you do, son," the doctor said.

"Oh, and why's that?"

"Our constable is not here for anyone other that Ben Kennard. In fact he's nothing more than one of Kennard's hired hands. He wasn't elected, he was appointed as constable, by none other than Kennard himself. Eden belongs to Ben Kennard. Well, everything that makes money, that is," the doctor said evenly.

"Does that include the local doctor," Brent asked seriously?

"No, it does not. He might think he owns me, but I've seen too many Ben Kennard types. He thinks he's above the law and tramples anyone under foot who gets in his way. You might say I'm the one thorn in his flesh," the doctor said with a grin.

"I see. Where's this Kennard's ranch, anyway," Brent asked?

The doctor gave him a long look before answering, "Are you intending to do to him what you just did to Waco and Luther in there," he said motioning towards the office "Because if you are, I can't in all good conscience, give you directions to his ranch. I would either be sending you to your death, him to his, or both of you to an early grave."

"He's got to pay for what he did. People can't just go around killing people wantonly," Brent said, thinking only about Julia's ordeal.

"That's what people say about every crime committed. Isn't that why we have lawmen? Some people do naturally what the law commands, while others almost take pleasure in breaking the law. You see, laws weren't made for the law abiding citizens; they're made for the lawbreakers. That's why you have to set a punishment for breaking the law," the doctor said as he worked over Julia.

"That's right. And there's a law about murdering people; and the punishment is death. Let's just say that I'm the hangman in this instance and Kennard is the killer," Brent replied.

"If I was you, I'd turn this over to a US Marshal and let him deal with Ben Kennard. That way you're clear of any wrong doing," the doctor stated.

Julia had not said much during the two men's conversation. Now she felt she should.

"I just want to get as far away from Ben Kennard as I possibly can. He will answer for his crimes; if not here when he stands before the Lord," Julia said.

Brent didn't say anything. He had heard his mother say that same thing more times than he could count. It hit home a little more when Julia said it, though. He felt somewhat unworthy of the feelings he'd been having for Julia after her statement. He couldn't help but wonder what kind of a man John Summers was?

The doctor looked at the lash marks on Julia's back and commented, "Did they use a bull whip on you, Ma'am?"

"Yes, the man riding the pinto did," Julia said.

The doctor looked up with a serious look on his face, "Waco rides a pinto," he said.

"Which one was he," Brent asked?

"He was the one I was attending to; the one who tried to use me as a shield. I asked him how he got those scratch marks on his face and he said a cat had scratched him," the doctor commented.

"I scratched the man who...., the man on the pinto. When I did is when he jumped up and shot me," Julia said as tears filled her eyes again.

"I'd like for you to stay at our house tonight, my dear. I wouldn't want infection to set in and I can check it in the morning and change the bandage," the doctor stated.

"Good," Brent said from outside the wagon. "I can stay right here in the wagon. That way I'll be close by if you need me for anything," Brent said readily.

"It wouldn't be that you'll be here should Ben Kennard find out she's staying here, could it," the doctor asked?

"That's a distinct possibility, Doc," Brent said with a wry grin. "Has Kennard done things like this before? I mean, these people were simply crossing his land. They weren't looking to homestead. From what I learned they were told by him that they had forty eight hours to get off his land.

"When they had a problem with a wheel on one of the wagons, they thought he would be understanding about their situation and give them a little more time. But, when the forty eight hours were up, he kills them all but Mrs. Summers. These folks were on their way up to some place around Lubbock, so why do what he did?"

The doctor nodded knowingly, "If Kennard gives his men an order they'll carry it out without asking any questions. It's my guess he told them the time was up and sent them out to make sure they were off his land. The men probably just became crazed over something and went too far."

"He went too far, and he'll pay for it someday," Brent said firmly, and then added. "Where can I pull this wagon where it will be out of your way?"

"Just pull it around in back of my office. There's even a water pump back there if you should need to pump some water," the doctor said and then added. "Will you help me get those two bodies down to the local undertaker?"

"I'd be glad too. You never can tell, he might have more business than he can handle before this thing is over," Brent said with just a hint of a smile.

The doctor didn't laugh at Brent's comment. He saw a look in the young man's eyes that he had seen on other men's faces that were making a vow to themselves.

The doctor also knew that Ben Kennard would be coming into town that evening, because it was the last of the month and that meant payday for his ranch hands. Kennard always came into town and got liquored up with his 'boys', as he liked to call them.

He didn't want to be a party to a killing spree, and was troubled as to whether he should tell this young man about Kennard or not. Finally he decided it would be better not to say anything and maybe the young man would not find out that Kennard was in town.

Brian (BJ) Sackett rode hard until he was a good fifteen miles from Kerrville. He knew there was a small town another thirty miles or so away by the name of Segovia. He and AJ had stopped there once while down this way on a business trip. It wasn't much of a town, so hopefully he wouldn't have any trouble there.

Brian knew that there would be a posse on his trail if Buster Rawlings had anything to say about it. He also knew that once he got back to Abilene it would be much harder for Buster to have open ears to listen to his lies.

Making sure that he wasn't leaving too easy a trail to follow, Brian would ride off the main trail from time to time and take to a stream or rocky ground to make tracking more difficult. He had just ridden into a small creek that traversed the main trail when he saw smoke coming from just over the next rise.

He was in Comanche territory and any sign of smoke like this could spell trouble. He continued to ride in the creek until he reached a point where he could ride to the crest of the hill and get a better look at what was causing the smoke.

When he topped the hill he reined up. There was a freight wagon a good two hundred yards away that was burning along with some of its cargo. Brian saw one dead mule near the wagon and what appeared to be a man lying near the dead animal.

He drew his gun as he kicked his horse up and headed down to the grisly scene. As he neared the burning wagon he kept a sharp eye out for any lingering Comanche's who might still be in the area.

Riding up to where the man he assumed was the freight driver lay, he cast one more quick look around before stepping down off his horse. The man was dead all right; shot three times. There was no harness on the dead animal, so that more than likely meant the Indians had taken the other mules with them.

BJ walked over to one of the crates to see what the freighter had been hauling. Pulling one of the busted crate boards back he peered inside.

"Books," he said. "This sure wouldn't do the Comanche's any good," he said to himself.

"He walked over and looked in one of the other crates that was also marked 'Books' on the outside. This crate, however, was empty. There was not one single book in it. Why would the Indians take all the books from one crate and not from the other?

Suddenly BJ had an idea and hurried back to the dead freight wagon driver. He went through the man's pockets and found a pouch containing gold nuggets. He estimated the nuggets to be worth somewhere in the neighborhood of eight hundred to a thousand dollars.

It was obvious that this man was hauling something more useful to the Indians than books. He was probably a gun runner. BJ found something else in the man's pocket as well. It was a letter to the man's wife. He read it aloud.

"Dear Wanda,

I'm sorry for all the hardship I've caused you. I don't blame you for taking little Abby and going back to your folks. All my big plans have gotten me is a bad back and empty pockets. Hopefully this job I just took will put a few dollars in my pocket and I can send you some money. It's a dangerous job, and the man who hired me is a man not to be trusted. I'm writing this in the hopes that I'm still alive when you get it. If not I want you to know that I love you and I always have. Kiss little Abby for me and tell her that her daddy loves and misses her. Love, Jim."

BJ looked at the envelope and noticed the address; it read 'Wanda Thalheimer, C/O, General Delivery, Buffalo Gap'.

"That's just south of Abilene," BJ said when he read the name of the place. "I guess I can deliver this for you, pardner. I'm sure she'd like to know what happened to her husband. And I'll see to it that she gets this," he said, bouncing the pouch filled with gold nuggets in his hand.

12

BRENT WALKED to the door of the bedroom that the doctor and his wife had put Julia up in and looked in. Julia was lying on her back with her eyes closed. Brent stood at the door for several seconds merely watching her.

"I gave her a sedative so she would get some rest," the doctor said from behind Brent, causing him to look back.

"Do you think this could scar her mentally, Doc. I mean she had to watch her husband and two others murdered in cold blood; could it have had a permanent impact on her emotionally," Brent asked in a concerned tone.

"It's hard to say. It was traumatic, to be sure, but the way she seems to have handled it so far looks like she's a very strong minded woman."

"I hope so. She seems like a very...uh...I don't know...sweet woman," Brent said seeking the right word to describe her.

"She does at that. I take it you haven't known her very long."

"No, I'd never seen her before I rode up where the shootings had taken place. I'll see to it that she gets to where she's going. It's up around Lubbock is all I really know right now though."

"Well, I'd say she'll be able to travel either tomorrow or the next day. I don't want to send her away from here too soon."

"I thank you for that, Doc. Well, I'm going to go out and make me a place to sleep in the wagon. I'll see you in the morning," Brent said as he moved away from the door and put his hat on that he had been holding in his hands.

"Good night, young man. D'you know, you never have told me your name and I'm tired of calling you 'young man'. What is your name anyway?"

"Oh, it's Dan Burton; from uh, Abilene," Brent said.

"You can call me Doc," the doctor said with a chuckle. "I've been called that so much, I actually think it's my real name."

"Okay, Doc. See ya' in the morning," Brent said and walked outside.

From the doctor's house it was about one hundred and fifty yards to the only cantina in town. He could hear the sound of a guitar and decided to go there and have a couple of drinks. As he was walking towards the cantina, seven riders from the Crooked K were nearing the small town from the other end. Along with them was Ben Kennard.

Brent had just gotten his beer and sat down at a table when Kennard and his riders reined up in front of the cantina. The men entered the cantina loudly, laughing and talking, and pushed a couple of men out of the way who were standing at the small bar.

"Set 'em up, Juan. I'm buying the first two rounds for my boys," Kennard said and pounded the bar hard with his quirt.

Looking around Kennard spotted Brent seated in the corner by himself. The two men locked their stares on one another and held them for several long seconds. Finally

Kennard gave in and looked away. Brent continued to stare at the big rancher with an expressionless gaze.

Kennard cast a quick glance towards Brent every so often and finally had had enough of the hard stares he had gotten since entering the saloon. He turned around and put his elbows back on the bar as he said, "Do you find something interesting about me," he said loudly?

Brent didn't answer at first but continued his stare. It was long enough to make Kennard repeat his question.

"Are you deaf, cowboy? I asked you a question. Do you find something interesting about me?"

This time Brent answered, "Yeah, I do. I was just wondering how you remind me of a stack of 'cow pies' I saw down the road a ways."

Kennard's men all stood in complete silence at the remark made by the stranger. They all cast a quick glance at Kennard to see what his reaction would be to the obvious slur. He just stood there glaring at Brent.

Finally Kennard replied, "I guess you don't know who you're talking too."

Brent shook his head slowly and said, "I don't know and I don't care."

"My name is Ben Kennard; does that mean anything to you?"

"Not a thing," Brent again replied.

"I own the largest cattle ranch in these parts and I run this town. These men work for me and do whatever I tell them to do. If I told them to kill you right now, that's what they would do," Kennard said slowly, and then asked, "Now what do you think of that?"

Brent's eyes narrowed and he grinned slightly, "That wouldn't do you a whole lot of good, now would it?"

"What do you mean by that," Kennard asked?

"You'd be where two of your riders by the names of Waco and Luther are about now; in Hell," Brent said, the words coming sharp and hard.

Kennard's eyes opened wider, but quickly narrowed. "Do you mean to tell me you killed Waco and Luther? I don't think one man could take them both. What did you do, shoot 'em in the back?"

"They both went down facing me....just like you'll do, Kennard," Brent said as he slowly stood to his feet.

Brent carried a six shooter in his holster and one tucked under his belt. His steady gaze was still on Kennard, but he could see every one of Kennard's men. He figured to kill the first man to go for a gun and then kill Kennard.

No one moved a muscle or blinked an eye. The tension was so thick you could cut it with a knife. Eyes darted around the room, as Kennard's men waited for someone to make a move.

Just then the cantina door opened and the local constable walked in. He smiled widely when he saw Ben Kennard, but his smile dropped quickly when he saw and felt the tension.

"What's going on in here," the constable asked.

"We have a real bad hombre, here, Edgar, a real bad hombre," Kennard said with a forced grin. "He's threatened to kill me. In fact, he said he killed Waco and Luther. Do you know anything about that?"

"Killed Luther and Waco...no, I didn't know that. When did that happen," the constable asked curiously?

"It would have had to have been today, ain't that right, stranger," Kennard asked Brent?

Brent nodded his answer.

"Where did the shootings take place? Both them boys were good with their guns," the constable went on?

"Where is it you're supposed to have gunned my boys down," Kennard questioned?

"Just down the street at the doctor's office. One of them was riding a big pinto and having some scratch marks on his face looked at by the doctor. Scratch marks I might add that he got from the woman he tried to kill," Brent said, his eyes narrowing.

One of the men to Kennard's right whispered, "That would have been Waco."

"Well, Edgar, what are you waiting for; I want this man arrested for murder," Kennard said to the constable.

Edgar looked from Kennard to Brent and started to draw his pistol from its holster. When he reached, so did one of Kennard's men.

Brent drew his holstered pistol and the one in his belt at the same time and started firing. Bullets flew from both sides of the small bar room. Men started dropping to the floor, either wounded or dead. One of the first to go down was the constable, followed next by Ben Kennard.

Brent had kicked the table he had been seated at over, and was using it as a shield, as he fired accurately and deadly. Two of the men who had not been shot yet, dropped their weapons and held up their hands.

"Don't shoot, Mister; don't shoot. We're not about to die when it looks like the one who pays us is dead," one of the men said.

Brent slowly stood up and moved across the room. He watched the men on the floor to make sure no one was merely playing dead. Kennard lay there with his eyes wide open and staring blankly up at the ceiling. The constable lay face down.

Brent looked at the two men with their hands in the air and asked, "Were you with the ones that killed the folks in the wagons yesterday?"

The two men looked at one another and then back at Brent. One of the men slowly shook his head yes and said, "But we didn't shoot anyone. That was done by the others."

Brent looked at each man coldly and started to lower his guns, but suddenly raised them again and said, "You could have stopped the others, but chose not too."

With that he fired two shots that dropped both men to the floor. They both lay there for just a couple of seconds before letting out a low moan and dying.

"You did nothing," Brent said under his breath.

As Brian rode along he wondered who the gun runner's wife was staying with in the Buffalo Gap area. He knew a number of the ranchers up there, but none by the name of Thalheimer. He did remember hearing a friend of his father's who had a ranch in that area, speak of his daughter Wanda. He wondered if they may be her family.

It was obvious that the man's wife was not aware of her husband's actions. In fact, according to the letter, he had never done anything like this before. Money will make people do some crazy things, BJ thought. Look at his own brother, Brent; it had certainly corrupted him.

Something caused BJ to look back over his shoulder. On a small rise about five hundred yards away was a Comanche war party. It wasn't a big one, but it was big enough. BJ wasted no time in kicking his horse into a full run. He knew now he would have to head for a settlement somewhere. He just hoped his horse wasn't too worn out from the long journey he'd been on.

BJ felt that the main trail was the best place to stay close too. If there was a cavalry patrol out here, the main trail is more than likely where they would be. Even a stagecoach would be a welcome sight, he thought. Anything or anyone that would add to his firepower would be fine.

The Indian's horses were fresher than BJ's and since the Indians didn't use saddles, their horses carried lesser weight. Each time he looked back he could tell the war party was gaining on him; slowly, but surely.

BJ patted the side of his horse's neck as it moved along the trail. After about a mile and a half he could feel his horse begin to slow. It was time to find a place to make a stand, but where. Again, he looked back, but this time it was to get an accurate count of the number of braves in the war party. He counted six.

Spotting a small arroyo off to his left he reined his tiring horse towards it. He just might be able to lose the Indians in it if it was like some he'd seen. By the time he reached the throat of the arroyo, the Indians were only about two hundred and fifty yards behind him.

Fortunately, the arroyo had been ravaged by flash flooding over the years and erosion had caused it to have smaller arroyos inside the major one. This could definitely work to his advantage.

BJ knew he would have to eventually leave his horse and began looking for the right place to make his stand. He rounded a bend and his heart almost leaped out of his chest.

Ahead of him, no more than fifty yards was another small war party; only this was a Kiowa war party. When they saw him they reacted totally opposite of what BJ thought they would. They rode their ponies up out of the arroyo and headed off to the east.

He was confused about the Indian's reaction until he heard the gunshots and saw the cavalry patrol. BJ reined his horse to a halt and grabbed his Winchester from its scabbard.

BJ waited until the first Comanche warrior rounded the bend in the arroyo and fired a carefully aimed shot that knocked the brave off the back of his horse. Another shot and another warrior hit the ground.

More gunshots followed, but these were from the cavalry troopers. Now it was the Indian's turn to try and out run the cavalry patrol. Both the Kiowa and Comanche war party's headed back to the south, but veered away from each other.

BJ watched the chase for a few moments and laughed with relief. When he glanced at one of the warriors he had shot he noticed something that caught his interest. It was the rifle that lay out in front of the downed Indian.

He led his horse over to where the rifle lay and picked it up. It was a new Winchester. This must have been one of the warriors who had taken the guns from Thalheimer. When BJ looked towards the dead brave, he noticed something shiny around the man's neck.

BJ walked over and saw that the shiny object was a locket on a chain. He slipped the chain from around the Indian's neck and opened the locket. There was a photograph of a woman and a small child.

On closer observation, BJ saw the two sets of initials engraved on the back of the locket. They were 'WT' and 'AT'.

BJ looked at the initials and said softly, "Wanda Thalheimer and Abby Thalheimer. So that's what you look like."

13

BRENT AND JULIA gave the doctor and his wife a wave as they pulled away from the doctor's house. Once the wagon had rounded the corner of the house the doctor and his wife turned and went inside.

"That young man is torn between good and evil. He has lead a violent life, but I think he wants to change. And I think the young woman may be the major reason he wants to change," the doctor said.

"It doesn't take a medical degree to figure that out. He's in love with her and it is written all over his face. I noticed it that very first day. He's protective of her, you'll have to agree with that," his wife said.

"I'd say so. That must have been some shootout in the cantina night before last. I'm glad they got out of here before a US Marshal came through and started investigating the shootings. That young Burton must be living under a lucky star. How he could shoot it out with Kennard and all of his men, and the constable, as well, and walk away without a scratch, is beyond me," the doctor said as he scratched his head.

"What are you going to tell a US Marshal if one comes around? Are you going to tell him the name of the man responsible for the killings?"

The doctor thought for a moment before saying, "Yes, I cannot lie for him. But I will say that I know for a fact, that Waco and Luther went for their guns first when they realized he was here with the woman they thought they'd killed. And from what Juan the bartender says, Kennard's men went for their guns first as well.

"I think the fact that Ben Kennard's men were responsible for the murders of the young lady's husband and the others will be enough to put Dan Burton in the clear."

Brent looked back at Julia as she lay in the bed he'd made for her in the wagon just behind the driver's bench seat. She had not heard of the shootings; the doctor and his wife had made sure of that. She was still suffering from the shock of her ordeal; but like the doctor said, she was a strong minded woman. Still, however, she would have a moment when she would breakdown, but not for long.

As they rode along Brent made small talk, but kept it interesting. He told her about beautiful scenery he had seen in different parts of the country where he'd traveled. Julia had never ventured far from where she had been born; in fact, the move to the small town of Sundown was her first real move of any distance.

"So how'd your husband happen to choose Sundown to start his cattle ranch," Brent asked?

"We knew a family who had moved up that way and they told us the owner had died and even though it was a small ranch, it was still too large for his wife. They didn't have any children, so she was going to move into the town of Lubbock," Julia said softly.

"Oh, I see. Well, I know quite a bit about ranching. I was raised on a cattle ranch and was herding cattle from the time I could sit a horse. I'd be glad to help you get started and settled in on your ranch. If you plan on keeping it, that is," Brent said honestly.

"Right now I don't know what to do. John paid the man when he and his brother went up to take a look at it. Do you think I should keep it, or should I try and sell it," Julia asked?

Brent thought for a moment and then said, "Why not wait until I have a chance to see it and then I'll tell you what I think?" As an after thought he said, "I'd be more than glad to stay on as your foreman. I could make sure anyone who went to work for you knew what they were doing."

"Would you do that for me?"

"Sure; why not; I'm between jobs," Brent smiled.

Julia grew quiet and Brent was afraid she was drifting back in thought to the day of the attack by Kennard's men and started to say something. Julia spoke before he had a chance to, however.

"You are a Godsend, Dan Burton; a true Godsend. If you hadn't come along when you did, I'd be dead. I don't know what happened in your past to bring you that way when you did, but it had to be the Hand of God guiding you," she said thoughtfully.

Brent lowered his head thinking back to why he was even in the area. He couldn't tell her that God would not have had him robbing and killing to bring him there. The hand of fate had to have been by mere chance, he thought. Brent knew that one day he would have to confess to Julia what his real name was and that he was nothing more than an outlaw. He'd have to one day, but this was not that day.

Carla Baskin sat at the table with Black Jack Haggerty with a half grin on her face. Jack glanced from her to Frank Jordan and then back at her.

"So how'd you find out my name," Jack asked?

Carla opened her handbag and pulled a folded up piece of paper out and handed it to Haggerty. He opened it up and looked at a wanted poster with his likeness on it. A half smile came to his face as he folded it back up and handed it back to Carla.

"Where'd you get that," he asked?

"Off the wanted poster board in front of the sheriff's office," she replied. "I thought you might not want your picture right out in plain sight where just anybody could see it," she said smugly.

"So what is it you want, Carla," Haggerty asked?

"You're no investor, so your interest in the bank across the street has to mean that you're planning on robbing it. I want in on it. I've lived in this one horse town long enough and I want a stake so I can move to San Francisco. You're going to provide me with that stake," Carla said seriously.

"We could just kill you," Jordan said evenly.

Carla shook her head, "I don't think so. I've taken precautions on that possibility. If anything happens to me you'll never get at that bank's money. Once that money is in your possession, you're going to drop ten thousand dollars off at a certain spot along your escape route. That will be my share," Carla said pointedly.

"You've got this all thought out, don't you, gal," Haggerty said.

"Uh, huh," she said shaking her head slowly up and down.

"And what if we don't throw the money off at the spot where you say," Haggerty asked?

Three Days to Sundown

"Then the man who'll have the rifle trained on you will shoot both of you out of the saddle and will be hailed a hero by the town's people," she said coyly.

The two men looked at one another and knew that she held the upper hand. They couldn't take the chance on doing anything to arouse suspicion before the money came in, which they had found out would be in two, maybe three days.

"I take it you've laid out a plan," Carla asked?

"Yeah, we have a plan...of course, it didn't include you up until a few seconds ago," Haggerty said.

"Well, I've got a plan for you that can't fail," Carla said self assuredly.

"Oh, is that right. Well then, let's hear this all fired can't fail plan of yours," Haggerty said casting a quick glance at Jordan.

"Abercrombie has been coming in here and having his Brandy with me for over a year. I know what he wants, but I wasn't about to give it up for just a few bucks; so I've played him like you would a wise old catfish. I'll let him think I'm ready to give in and tell him to meet me in my friend's place near the livery stable. You be waiting when we get there and force him to go to the bank and open it up. You can do it before it opens and no will be the wiser until the bank opens and they find Harvey bound and gagged in his chair. You'll be long gone and he won't be able to tell the truth about what happened for fear of his wife finding out about him and me.

"And of course you'll drop ten thousand dollars off on your way out of town. My friend will have you covered at one end of town and I'll have you covered at the other. Oh, and let me warn you boys; I'm a crack shot with a rifle. You can ask anyone in Sundown and they'll tell you that I've won several turkey shoots over the years," Carla grinned.

137

Haggerty nodded slowly as he took in her idea for the robbery. He liked the part about no one being alerted until the bank had opened. They could be miles away from town before the alarm was sounded. The more he thought about it the more he liked it. All but the part about the ten thousand dollars, that is.

"Carla, you just bought into a bank robbery," Haggerty said. "How will we know when to pull it off?"

"I'll tell you the day before the money gets here for deposit. I'm friends with the bank president remember. And I know it isn't coming in tomorrow," Carla said with a chuckle.

Haggerty looked at Carla with a cold, hard look for several seconds, but then began to grin, which soon gave way to a full blown smile, followed by a belly laugh. Jordan looked at Haggerty with a confused look on his face.

"What's so funny, Jack," Jordan asked?

"This woman," Haggerty said nodding towards Carla. "We should have had her planning all of our jobs," he added.

Carla grinned at Haggerty and then looked at Jordan, who wasn't laughing.

"That is a great plan," Haggerty said as he shook his head in approval. "This gal would make a great poker player. She's got patience and brains."

Carla looked wounded, "You didn't say anything about charm, good looks, or sex appeal?"

"Yeah, yeah, but I like the brains and patience better," Haggerty said still chuckling.

Brent Sackett helped Julia down out of the wagon and seated her near the campfire he had built. Once she was seated he placed a blanket over her shoulders.

"These nights out here can get a little cool. I hope you like what I rustled up for supper," Brent said as he dished up some of the stew that the doctor's wife had sent along.

Julia smiled, "You only heated it. I know the doctor's wife sent that along."

Brent looked at her and returned the smile. "That's the first time I've seen you smile," he said.

Julia lowered her gaze, "I haven't felt much like smiling or laughing. To be honest, it felt good to smile again. One day I'll be back to normal I hope."

"Of course you will. Now try some of this and tell me if I did a good job of heating it," Brent said with a chuckle.

"I'm sure you did," Julia said as she took the plate and held it in her lap. Taking a spoon full of the stew she said, "Mm, this is the best heated stew I've ever tasted."

Brent laughed as he shoveled a spoonful into his mouth, "I think you're right. Whoever heated this stew knew what they were doing."

Brent Sackett was in love. He'd never been in love before. He'd been with his share of women, but all he'd felt for them was lust. His feelings for Julia was different from anything he'd ever felt before. He knew now that he had fallen deeply in love with her. He hoped that someday she'd feel the same towards him.

"Mrs. Summers, I was wondering if it would be all right with you if I called you by your first name," Brent asked politely.

Julia looked at him and smiled again, "I don't see why not. If I may call you Dan, that is?"

"I'd be honored...but I'd be even more honored if you'd call me Brent."

"Is that your middle name," Julia asked?

"No it's my first name," Brent said truthfully.

"Then Brent it is."

"Okay, Julia...Julia, that has got to be one of the prettiest names I've ever heard," Brent grinned.

Julia took another bite of her stew and thought for a moment before asking her next question. After she'd chosen the words she wanted to say, she spoke up, "What happened back in that town of Eden that you don't want me to know about?"

Brent looked up quickly into her face, "Why, what makes you ask that question?"

"I know that something happened at the doctor's office the day we arrived there. I vaguely remember hearing gunshots. What were the gunshots about," she asked?

Brent had wondered why she had never brought it up about the gunshots she would have had to have heard if she wasn't unconscious. He wondered how she would handle the truth, and he was about to find out.

"When we got to the doctor's office two of the men involved in the shooting were there. One was the man riding the pinto you told me about," he paused, choosing his words carefully. "Well, when I called them out about what they had done to you folks; they went for their guns. I had no choice but to shoot them both.

"I don't know if you were aware of it, or not, but the town constable worked for Ben Kennard, so I couldn't go to him about the shootings. The doctor was a witness to the whole thing. One of the men even tried to use the doctor as a shield to hide behind."

Julia's eyes widened as she listened to Brent's account of the shooting. When he had finished she asked thoughtfully, "Then the man who attacked and shot me is...dead!"

"I figure he's hot footing around Hell about now, yeah," Brent replied.

Julia looked down and when she looked back up into Brent's eyes, had tears in her own.

"I've been having terrible nightmares about that man. I've seen his face every night since the shootings," she said and paused. "Maybe now I can get some real rest."

"I knew you were having nightmares," Brent replied. "You cried out in your sleep several times. I'd wake you, but you'd go right back to sleep."

"Then you were the one on the white horse I would see riding up from behind the man who was attacking me in my dream," Julia said as her eyes widened slightly. "At the end of every dream I could see a distant rider drawing closer and closer. He never got close enough for me to see his face, but it must have been you."

"Dreams are funny things," Brent smiled. "I have some crazy ones. Once I dreamed I was sitting in church with no clothes on," he said with a slight chuckle.

"I've had dreams similar to that. I asked our preacher about it and he said he really didn't know what it meant, but it could be that when people stand before God all the outer is stripped away and he looks on a person's heart. He sees the inside of a person and is not fooled by what they want others to see," Julia replied.

Brent nodded slightly, "That makes a lot of sense," he said and then paused. "So you and your husband were church going people, huh?"

"Yes, just about every Sunday. We had a very good preacher. He didn't preach a lot of 'hellfire and brimstone' messages like so many others do. Oh, he talked about Hell and that only those who denied God would go there, but he spoke mostly about the love of God," Julia said thoughtfully.

Brent hadn't even thought about the Lord for years, other than an occasional taking of His name in vain. Suddenly he felt a condemnation unlike anything he'd ever felt in his life. He couldn't put his finger on what it was, except that he felt dirty. Not dirty physically, but dirty inside. The feeling truly bothered him.

"Well, we'd better get to sleep if we're going to get an early start in the morning. I figure we'll get into Sundown around noon," Brent said changing the subject, but still somewhat bothered by the thoughts he'd just had.

Julia looked at Brent for a moment and said softly, "I'm not sure if I'm glad or sad about that."

"I don't want you to worry about anything. Everything's going to work out all right; you'll see. Hey, where's your faith," Brent said with a smile?

"Brent, I have to tell you something that I think you should know," Julia said and then paused before going on. "I wasn't happy in my marriage to John. He was a very controlling man. He was a good man, I guess, but was so demanding in what he expected of me. Therefore, I can't say I'm sorry the marriage has ended; I just don't like the way it ended. I certainly didn't hate him; and I never wanted to see him dead.

"Our marriage was more a matter of convenience than love. John needed a wife and I was the only woman around that was in his age range. He was ten years older than me. Once in awhile he would get drunk and once he hit me. I told him if he ever did it again, I'd leave him. He never did, although I know he wanted to several times. I just thought I should tell you that."

Brent listened quietly and when she was finished with her confession, took a deep breath. Before speaking he wrestled with the thought of making a few confessions of his own. Finally he decided against telling her that he was a man on the run. He was afraid he might lose her if he did; and he didn't want to lose her. He'd wait until he knew their relationship was strong enough to handle the whole truth. If it ever was, that is.

14

CARLA SMILED at Harvey Abercrombie as he told her that the largest bank deposit in the history of the bank would be arriving that night. She tried to act only somewhat interested as he boasted about what this would mean to the town of Sundown; and to him personally.

"So when the bank opens tomorrow the bank will have more money in it than it ever has," Carla asked as though she were having trouble grasping what he had just told her?

"Yes, I'll have to stay late tonight, until the money arrives. This is a big day for Sundown, believe me. This town will have some working capital to grow on. I hope the investors I talked to are still around, I have some ideas I'd like to run by them. You haven't seen them lately have you, Carla? They haven't been around for a day or two; at least I haven't seen them."

"I think they're still in the area. I only met them in here. If I see them I'll tell them you want to meet with them," Carla said and then paused before saying, "Harvey, I may be going away."

Harvey took on a surprised look, "What...why? Where are you going, Carla?"

"I got word that my mother back in St. Louis is ill and I may have to go back there to take care of her. I'm waiting for word from my sister now," she lied sadly.

"Oh, no; that's terrible news, Carla. Will you be coming back here to Sundown?"

"I don't know. I really have no reason to come back here. I hate this job I'm forced to do and I don't have many that I'm really close to here; other than you, that is. I know one thing, though. I'm going to miss you terribly. And I wish now that..., no never mind," she said turning her face away.

"Go ahead, Carla, you wish now, what?"

Carla looked down at her glass of Brandy and then looked up into Harvey's eyes, "I wish we had been....intimate."

Harvey's eyes widened at her statement, "Oh, I do too, Carla. You know I've always wanted to...well, to love you. Now don't get me wrong, I love Dora, my wife, but I've so wanted to love you too," he said dropping his voice slightly.

"I've been thinking about you more and more lately. I lie in my bed and...no; I can't say it. What would you think of me?"

"Go ahead Carla and get it off your chest. Don't keep your feelings all bottled up inside," Harvey encouraged.

"I guess you're right, since I may be leaving, what harm would my confession do? Please don't think badly of me, but I've lay in my bed and longed for you to be there with me," she said looking at him demurely.

"Oh, Carla...I've waited so long to hear those words from you. I, too, have longed for you and me to be entwined," Harvey said dreamily.

It was all Carla could do to keep from laughing, but she played her part perfectly.

"Would you think it a terrible thing if tonight," she started to say and then stopped before adding, "Oh, you can't tonight; the money shipment is coming in."

"Go ahead, Carla; what were you going to ask me? Please, go ahead and ask."

"I was just thinking that perhaps you could spend a few hours with me tonight. I'm expecting a telegram from my sister at anytime and when it comes I'll have to leave immediately. What if I never saw you again? I want to remember you in that way, Harvey," Carla smiled sweetly.

"Oh, me too, me too, Carla," Harvey cooed, and then said excitedly, "I know. I could come by your place after the money arrives and then tell Dora that I had to work late. Would that be to your satisfaction? I wouldn't know the exact time, but it will be around midnight, I'm sure."

"That would be fine with me, Harvey. This will be 'our night' together," Carla said tenderly.

Harvey looked around to make sure no one was listening to him before saying, "I know that the money should be arriving around ten o'clock tonight. It will take me a little while to do some necessary things with the bookkeeping, and then I'll stop by your place. It should be around midnight...I think they call that the 'bewitching hour'!"

"Oh, Harvey, you have such a way with words," Carla said with a titter.

"Well, I'd better get home and set the stage for our little rendezvous. Oh, Carla, you don't know what this means to me," Harvey said excitedly. "I'm beside myself with anticipation," he said as he cast a quick glance down at her ample cleavage.

"Same here...big boy," Carla said blushingly.

With one last schoolboy giggle, Harvey rushed to the door of the saloon, but before leaving looked back and gave Carla one more little wave. She waved back with a smile and he hurried on his way home.

Once Harvey had gone Carla jumped out of her chair and called to the bartender, "Joe, can I borrow your horse? I have to run an errand; I'll be back in about a half hour or so."

"Well, okay, don't be gone too long; and don't run him," Joe replied.

"I won't," Carla said and rushed out the door.

Haggerty had told Carla where he and Frank Jordan were staying, so she had no trouble finding the place. When she told Haggerty that the money would be arriving that night and that she had arranged for Abercrombie to come to her place around midnight, Haggerty laughed and slapped his knee.

"Woman, you are a natural born bank robber," Haggerty said. "Frank, I think we've found us a new member of our gang."

"What gang; we don't have one, remember," Jordan answered.

"We do now; a gang of three. Carla, I've got big plans for you," Haggerty said thoughtfully.

"Oh, is that right. Just remember about the ten thousand dollars you're to drop. If you're serious, you tell me where we can meet up and I'll be there. If you don't show up, it will be to your loss; because, I'll still have my money from this job," Carla said seriously.

"I can tell you right now where we'll meet up; in Amarillo," Haggerty said truthfully.

"Isn't that a little close to Sundown? I'd think you'd want to meet further away," Carla said with a frown.

"We'll be moving on from there. Have you ever been to Santa Fe, New Mexico?"

"No, have you," Carla asked?

"I've been everywhere, woman. I've got a little job in mind that could make this one look like peanuts. I've got a hankering for some silver," Haggerty laughed.

"Let's take care of one job at a time, shall we."

"I like you, Carla; I like you a lot," Haggerty grinned.

"You and Harvey Abercrombie," Carla laughed and then added quickly, "Now, getting back to tonight. You know where my place is, so give Harvey time to get there; he said around midnight. You bust in the door at around 1:00 in the morning. You won't have any trouble with the door, believe me. I don't want him to know I'm a part of this, so it will put me in the clear if you bust in on us.

"When you leave town go out passed the livery stable and you'll see a large wash tub right alongside the road. Toss this flour sack in it with the ten thousand dollars in it. If you don't, my friend will shoot you dead, believe me," Carla said with a frown.

She went on, "If you head out of town the other way, I'll shoot you down and you'll be just as dead. I don't take kindly to being played for a sucker; so don't even go there."

Haggerty grinned at the cleverness of this woman. She'd hatched a good plan in a short amount of time. He was serious, now, about making her part of his gang. Besides having a good head on her shoulders, she wasn't a bad looking woman.

"I like your idea; it's a go," Haggerty said.

Brian Sackett rode up to the small post office in Buffalo Gap. There was one trading post with a saloon, a blacksmith and a hardware/feed store. He pushed the door open and a pretty young woman looked up from her chair behind the counter and smiled.

"Hello," she said in a pleasant voice.

"Are you the postmaster here," Brian asked in a surprised voice?

"No, I'm just filling in for him for a few minutes; but I can help you," she said.

"I hope so. I'm looking for a Mrs. Thalheimer, a Mrs. Wanda Thalheimer; do you know her," Brian asked?

"What do you want with her," the woman asked curiously?

"I have a letter for her from her husband, I guess. The envelope had her name and c/o general delivery here in Buffalo Gap. I just wanted to make sure she gets it," Brian explained.

The woman nodded slight, "I'm Wanda Thalheimer."

Brian looked shocked at first, but then smiled, "I guess you can't get no more 'general delivery' than that, huh."

"May I have the letter, please," she asked, extending her hand.

"Oh, yeah....sure, here it is," Brian said and pulled the folded up letter from his coat pocket.

She took the letter with a smile and opened it up. As she read the letter her countenance changed to one of sadness. When she had finished reading it, she folded it back up and looked at Brian again.

"Did he give you this to deliver to me," she asked?

Brian paused slightly before replying, "No, I found it on his...," he paused again, "He was attacked by a Comanche war party."

Wanda tensed slightly at the news, knowing that her husband was dead. She closed her eyes and slowly shook her head from side to side.

"I was afraid something like this would happen. He had been so unlucky at life. Everything he tried seemed to fail," she said more to herself than to Brian. "Did he...suffer much?"

Brian shook his head no, "No, it was quick."

"Thank God for that," Wanda said as tears formed in her eyes.

Just then her father returned from the trading post. When he saw his daughter with tears in her eyes, he quickly eyed Brian.

"What is it, honey," he asked his daughter.

Three Days to Sundown

"This gentleman brought news from Jim. He was killed by a Comanche war party," Wanda said as a tear slowly trickled down her soft cheek.

"I'm sorry to be the bearer of bad news. I happened upon the wagon he had been driving and when I found the letter on him, I felt it only right to deliver it personally," Brian said quietly.

"Thank you, young man," Wanda's father said. "Jim would be thankful for that as well."

"Well, I'd better be getting on up to our ranch in Abilene. I'm sorry, Ma'am; I truly am," Brian said honestly.

Wanda looked at him and forced a smile, "Thank you, thank you."

She then turned her face away and began to weep softly. Brian felt it was time to leave her and her father alone. He sent outside and stopped and looked back towards the door before finally stepping up on his horse and heading for the Sackett ranch. He was only ten miles from home now.

Harvey Abercrombie scurried down the alley that led to Carla's rental. Looking around nervously he knocked on the door and waited impatiently until she opened up. He stepped inside giving one last peek outside to make sure he had not been spotted.

When he turned around his eyes widened as he beheld Carla standing there with a sheer gown under a long lounging robe which was opened at the top. His eyes wandered over her curvaceous body and he instinctively licked his lips.

He let out a low moan as Carla moved up and put her arms around him, kissing him passionately on the lips. The moan turned to a whimpering sound as his knees became weak with anticipation. Suddenly the room began to swim before his eyes as his heart beat faster and faster, until he finally fainted dead away.

"Oh, great," Carla said in disgust. "Here I was going to give you the night of your life and you faint on me."

Walking over to her table she picked up a pitcher of water and threw it into Abercrombie's face. He sat upright with a start, spitting and sputtering.

"Cough, cough...what happened," Harvey said as he blinked his eyes repeatedly?

"You fainted, Harvey. Are you all right, honey," Carla asked sweetly, but having to force herself to do so?

"Oh, my, I'm sorry. Everything started swimming and then the entire room went black. I hope you'll forgive me," Harvey said getting to his feet.

"Oh, you're all wet. You'll have to get out of those wet clothes before you catch your death of pneumonia," Carla said as she started unbuttoning his vest.

She wanted to get him in a compromising position before Haggerty and Jordan burst in on them. That way, Harvey would not expect she had anything to do with the robbers, and even if he suspected her, would not want to implicate her for fear of his wife finding out where he really was the night the bank was robbed.

"Oh," he said shyly.

"You just lay back on the bed and let me take care of the rest," Carla said.

Haggerty looked at his watch and then at Jordan, "It's time; let's go."

Jordan nodded but asked, "Are you really going to toss them ten thousand dollars?"

"It depends on how much is in the bank. If there's as much as they say is coming, yeah. If not, no. I trust Carla on that point. Besides, I like knowing where people are who might decide to take pot shots at me."

"I say we keep it all. How do we know there'll be someone watching the bank and that she'll be out by the livery stable," Jordan argued.

"I think she'll have someone posted at the bank and from what I've heard around town, she is a good shot with a rifle. I've got plans for her," Haggerty replied.

The two of them walked quietly up to Carla's front door and Haggerty put his ear up to the door. When he heard the moaning coming from inside he nodded to Jordan. They pulled their bandanas up over their nose to hide their face and Haggerty then threw his weight against the door, knocking it open, and he and Jordan burst into the room with guns drawn.

"Get up them hands," Jordan snapped as Abercrombie tried desperately to cover himself. Carla made a modest attempt, but still allowed a lot of exposure.

"Don't shoot, don't shoot," Abercrombie yelled, thinking at first it might be suitors of Carla's. Once the realization set in that these men were robbers his attitude changed.

"Get your clothes on and be quick about it," Jordan ordered.

"Please don't hurt us," Carla said, playing her role to the hilt.

"Shut up. You do as you're told and everything will be all right,' Jordan said.

Haggerty had decided to remain quiet because he had done most of the talking to the bank president and his voice would be more recognizable to the man.

"What are you going to do," Harvey asked?

"You're going to open up that bank of yours, but only to us two new customers. We want to make a little withdrawal of our money," Jordan said sarcastically.

"You're going to rob the bank; you can't fool me," Harvey said, causing the two men to look at one another in somewhat disbelief.

"You're too smart for me. Yes, that's exactly what we're going to do," Jordan snapped, and then added quickly, "Get those clothes on."

Once Abercrombie was dressed they pushed him towards the door and told Carla to stay where she was. Haggerty went out with the bank president and Jordan paused and said, "I'll take care of the woman."

Haggerty disguised his voice and said, "Tie her up."

"Yeah, sure," Jordan said and moved Carla away from the doorway.

Once they were out of view of Haggerty and Abercrombie, Jordan hit Carla over the head with his gun, knocking her out. Looking down at her he said quietly, "Let's see you shoot us out of the saddle now."

They took Abercrombie to the bank where they made him open up the back door so no one would see them entering. He resisted when they told him to open the safe, but when Jordan put a gun to his head and jacked the hammer back, Harvey gave in.

"You'll never get away with this," he said as he turned the handle and opened the safe's door. "They'll find you."

Jordan snapped, "They'll have to go to Mexico to do it."

With Jordan holding his pistol on Abercrombie, Haggerty shoved the money into two large pillow cases. He knew there had to be in excess of a hundred fifty thousand dollars.

"We've hit a bonanza," Haggerty said in his excitement.

Abercrombie looked at Haggerty and his eyes widened, "You're...." he started to say but never finished his sentence before Jordan hit him over the head and knocked him unconscious.

Haggerty saw and barked, "What did you do that for? We might need him."

"I doubt it," Jordan said. "Now him and Carla can nurse each other's aching heads."

"You knocked her out, too? I wanted her for our next job, Frank," Haggerty snapped angrily.

"Then toss her a bone...ten thousand of them. She'll have an alibi if she has a knot on her head," Jordan said unconcernedly.

"Yeah, I guess you're right."

They took the money and hightailed it out the back door of the bank to where they had left their horses earlier. Haggerty wondered if Carla really had someone watching the bank. They headed out of town in the direction of the livery stable so there were no shots fired.

As they rode Haggerty pulled a small bag out from under his coat and stuffed a wad of bills into it. When they passed the washtub on the side of the road, he tossed the bag into it. He didn't know if there was ten thousand, but it would be enough to get Carla to Amarillo.

They rode all through the night. The sun was just peeking over the distant horizon when they saw the lone covered wagon and smelled the aroma of coffee brewing. Haggerty looked at Jordan, "Chow time," he said.

They rode up to the wagon and were greeted by Brent Sackett. Haggerty spoke first as they reined their horses to a halt.

"That coffee sure smells good," Haggerty said with a grin.

"Get down and have a cup," Brent said warily.

When Brent looked at Jordan the two of them recognized each other immediately.

"Sackett," Jordan said as he went for his gun.

Brent beat Jordan to the draw and fired first. His bullet hit Jordan in the shoulder of his gun hand, causing him to drop his pistol. Haggerty, taken by surprise, had time to pull his revolver and fire a snap shot that hit Brent in the chest area. He went down hard, but managed to get a shot off that hit Haggerty in the side.

Haggerty started to finish Brent off when a rifle shot rang out. The bullet shattered Haggerty's saddle horn, causing him to look towards the one doing the shooting. It was Julia. Haggerty and Jordan kicked their horses up and rode off in a cloud of dust.

Julia rushed to Brent's aid and fell to the ground by his side. She cradled his head in her lap and rocked back and forth. Brent was in bad shape. His wound was serious. Julia prayed that he would not die and began trying to get him into the back of the wagon.

Finally with a little help from Brent she got him aboard and headed for the town of Sundown. She prayed she would be able to find a doctor once she arrived in town. As she drove the team of horses hard, she looked down at the man she was beginning to feel a real fondness for and prayed he would not die.

The sign said fifteen miles. Would she make it in time; it was hard to say. The wound was serious and Brent's breathing was labored. If he could just hold on, she thought.

In his unconscious state Brent looked as though he were at peace with the world. He was, but it was to be at peace with God that mattered most. In his dreams he was running through green fields with Julia holding his hand.

Julia whipped the horses, getting as much speed out of them as possible. She forgot totally about her wound and the jarring that she was taking place. She didn't notice that her own wound had reopened. She was too concerned about Brent. She closed her eyes and said to herself, "Next stop, Sundown."

The End

Watch for the next episode: "Ride the Hard Land"

Three Days to Sundown

Raymond D. Mason

Printed in Great Britain
by Amazon